THE SECRET EXPLORERS
3 BOOKS IN 1

Penguin
Random
House

THIS EDITION
Editorial Kritika Gupta, Syed Tuba Javed   **Design** Rashika Kachroo
Special Sales and Custom Publishing Executive Issy Walsh
Managing Editor Monica Saigal   **Managing Art Editor** Romi Chakraborty
DTP Designer Dheeraj Singh   **Production Editor** Becky Fallowfield
Production Controller Mandy Inness   **Delhi Creative Head** Malavika Talukder
Deputy Art Director Mabel Chan   **Publisher** Francesca Young
Publishing Director Sarah Larter

ORIGINAL EDITIONS
For Conall, space expert and voyager among the stars
(*The Secret Explorers and the Comet Collision*)

For Eddie Beard (*The Secret Explorers and the Tomb Robbers*)

Design by Collaborate Ltd   **Illustrator** Ellie O'Shea
Consultants Derek Harvey (*The Secret Explorers and the Lost Whales*), Sophie Allan
(*The Secret Explorers and the Comet Collision*) Angela MacDonald
(*The Secret Explorers and the Tomb Robbers*),
Acquisitions Editor Sam Priddy   **Senior Commissioning Designer** Joanne Clark
US Editorial Shannon Betty, Margaret Parrish
Senior Production Editor Nikoleta Parasaki
Senior Producer Ena Matagic   **Publishing Director** Sarah Larter

First American Edition, 2023
Published in the United States by DK Publishing
1745 Broadway, 20th Floor, New York, NY 10019

Content previously published in:
The Secret Explorers and the Lost Whales (2020)
The Secret Explorers and the Comet Collision (2020)
The Secret Explorers and the Tomb Robbers (2020)

Text copyright © 2020, 2023 Working Partners
Layout copyright © 2020, 2023 Dorling Kindersley Limited
DK, a Division of Penguin Random House LLC
23 24 25 26 27 10 9 8 7 6 5 4 3 2 1
001–340436–Aug/2023

A catalog record for this book
is available from the Library of Congress.
ISBN: 978-0-7440-9727-6

DK books are available at special discounts when purchased in bulk for sales promotions,
premiums, fund-raising, or educational use. For details, contact: DK Publishing Special Markets,
1745 Broadway, 20th Floor, New York, NY 10019
SpecialSales@dk.com

Printed and bound in Huizhou, Guangdong Province, China

All images © Dorling Kindersley Limited

For the curious
www.dk.com

MIX
Paper | Supporting
responsible forestry
FSC™ C018179

This book was made with Forest
Stewardship Council™ certified
paper—one small step in DK's
commitment to a sustainable future.
**For more information go to
www.dk.com/our-green-pledge**

The publisher would like to thank: Sally Beets, James Mitchem, and Seeta Parmar
for editorial assistance; Sonny Flynn and Charlie Milner for design assistance;
and Caroline Twomey for proofreading.

CONTENTS

Text for DK by Working Partners Ltd
9 Kingsway, London WC2B 6XF
With special thanks to Adrian Bott (*The Secret Explorers and the
Comet Collision* and *The Secret Explorers and the Tomb Robbers*) and
Valerie Wilding (*The Secret Explorers and the Lost Whales*)

THE SECRET EXPLORERS AND THE LOST WHALES

Chapter One
POND DIPPING

Connor dipped his net into the pond and scooped up a big clump of algae. Long green strands of the tiny plants trailed down. It looked like Connor had caught a watery monster. *I guess I have*, he thought. After all, too much algae would block out the light, and the other plants in the pond would die.

Connor had spent the morning clearing

up the water. The pond was at the end of his backyard, on the other side of the white picket fence. The leaves of the pecan trees gleamed in the warm Missouri sunshine.

Connor dropped the algae onto the bank. He was about to scoop out another clump, when he noticed something wriggling inside the net. A tadpole!

"Hey, there!" said Connor. "Are you going to grow into a bullfrog? Or maybe a leopard frog?" Gently, he lowered the net so the tadpole could escape. He watched it swim away, kicking its tiny back legs. It joined a large group of tadpoles beside some reeds.

Hold on, Connor thought. *They're hanging out in a shoal... Those probably aren't frog tadpoles—I think they're toads!*

Connor loved everything about the water. His mom thought he would be a marine biologist when he grew up and study the plants and animals in the sea.

"We'll have to take a vacation to the coast one day," Mom had said at breakfast. "Wouldn't it be amazing to see the ocean?"

Connor touched the compass badge on his chest. His mom didn't know that Connor had seen lots of oceans already...

When he'd scooped out the last gloopy blob of algae, Connor propped his net against the wooden fence. It was hot now. The sunshine shimmered on the wheat fields that surrounded his house. Connor made his way indoors.

He washed his hands at the kitchen sink, then went to the pantry to get himself a granola bar. There was a postcard tacked to the pantry door. It said, "I Love Missouri Science Fair!" Connor had won first prize in the competition for growing coral in a tank.

As he reached for the door handle, he stopped in surprise.

A glowing shape had appeared next to the postcard.

 It was a circle with a needle in the center. Around the outside were the letters N, S, E, and W.

A compass!

A compass that matched the badge on Connor's T-shirt...

Connor grinned. *The Secret Explorers have a new mission!* he thought.

Excitement tingled through him as he stepped through the door. The shelves of food were gone, and instead there was a dazzling white light. Connor's heart thudded. Wind whipped against his face, as if he were traveling really fast...

A moment later, the light faded. Connor was standing in a large, familiar room. Light from the rows of computer screens flickered on the black stone walls. Objects stood on display in glass cabinets, just like in a museum. There were dinosaur fossils, meteorites from space, and shells from the bottom of the ocean. On the floor was a huge map of the world. The domed ceiling showed the stars and the Milky Way. Connor was back in the Exploration Station!

"Connor—here!" he said.

Near the computers was a cluster of comfy chairs. A girl with short dark hair jumped up from one of them. A compass badge just like Connor's was pinned to her soccer jersey.

"Hey, Tamiko!" said Connor. He noticed her cool Stegosaurus necklace—Tamiko's specialty subject was dinosaurs.

"Hi!" Tamiko said. "Look—here come the others!"

The rest of the Secret Explorers began to hurry through the glowing doorway. A tall, grinning girl gave a salute, just like she always did. "Leah—here!" she called. Leah knew everything about plants and animals.

Next came Kiki, who loved machines and technology. She wore glasses and pajamas, and her hair was still ruffled from sleep.

"Kiki—here!"

"Ollie—here!" said a red-haired boy in a rain forest T-shirt.

The rest of the team called out their names. There was Roshni, who wanted to be an astronaut, Gustavo who loved history, and Cheng who knew everything about rocks and volcanoes.

The roll call was complete. Connor was buzzing with excitement—now they would be given their mission! Everyone took their usual place around the map on the floor.

Sure enough, a circle of light glimmered on part of the map. Connor recognized where it was right away—the South Pacific Ocean, to the east of Australia. The circle got bigger. It became the size of a TV screen. It showed a pod of whales diving through the water. They had long fins and white bellies.

"Humpback whales," said Connor.

But who would the Exploration Station choose for this adventure? It always picked the two members with the right skills and knowledge for the mission.

Connor looked down to see his compass badge glowing with light. "I'm in!" he cried. He was the club's marine expert, so that made sense. But who would be his teammate? Roshni's badge shimmered, lighting up her face.

"Cool!" Roshni said. "But my specialty is space. I wonder what that's got to do with humpback whales?"

"I guess we'll find out," said Connor. He gave her a high five. "The Exploration Station is never wrong!"

Kiki pressed a button on one of the computers. A vehicle with two seats rose up from the floor. "The Beagle, ready to go," Kiki said. The Beagle was named after a ship sailed by the famous scientist Charles Darwin. It looked like an old go-kart, with chipped paint and a crooked steering wheel.

But it's so much more than just a go-kart, Connor thought.

The other Secret Explorers took their places at the computers, ready to give Connor and Roshni any help they needed during their mission.

"Good luck!" called Cheng.

"Can't wait to hear all about it!" added Tamiko.

"Call us if you need anything!" said Kiki.

Connor and Roshni waved goodbye to their friends, then clambered into the Beagle. Connor gripped the steering wheel. "Ready?" he asked.

Roshni nodded. "Ready."

He leaned forward and pressed a button on the dashboard that said "START." The Beagle began to shake. The nuts and bolts shuddered as if they would pop out at any moment. There was a bright flash. The Beagle jerked forward, and Connor and Roshni were flung back against their seats. Suddenly, they were zooming through a tunnel of light.

Beneath them, the Beagle began to transform. The wheels slid away. A joystick replaced the steering wheel. Glass rose around them. "Maybe it's turning into a boat this time!" Connor cried, his voice trembling under the force.

There was a huge splash. Connor gazed out in wonder through a curved window. Blue water stretched as far as he could see.

Overhead flew a white tropic bird with long tail feathers.

"It's the Pacific Ocean!" he said.

Roshni pointed at a periscope sticking up through the glass ceiling of the cockpit.

"We're not in a boat," she said with a grin. "We're in a submarine!"

Chapter Two
THE SEARCH HEATS UP

A dashboard rose up from the Beagle's floor. Panels popped open to reveal screens and switches. The change was complete and the Beagle bobbed peacefully on the water.

"Look at all these controls!" Connor said excitedly. "What do you think they do?"

Roshni grinned. "Let's find out."

Every time the Beagle changed to a new

vehicle, it took on new special features. Figuring out what everything did was half the fun.

Connor pointed out a round screen with glowing green lights. "This must be the sonar," he said. "It uses sound waves to measure distances underwater."

"I think this is for navigation," said Roshni, who was peering into a display. "There's us, look, and there's the seabed under us. It's like a satnav."

In the cupboards under the dashboard were energy bars, water bottles, and two wet suits with masks and oxygen tanks.

"We can go on a dive!" Connor said. "Wait until you see the coral up close. It's amazing. So many colors. And the fish come right up to you!"

"We'd better find the whales first," Roshni replied.

"For sure," Connor agreed.

They were here to help, he reminded himself. They didn't yet know what sort of help the whales needed, but the Exploration Station had sent them here for a reason.

Roshni turned her seat to face the sonar screen. "Why don't you drive and I'll work the instruments?"

"Cool!"

Connor gripped the joystick with one

hand and the depth control with the other. He slowly brought the Beagle down below the surface. Lapping water rose around the glass bubble.

Down in the green depths, everything was much quieter. Waves danced above them like a silver sheet. Light slanted down in faint rays. Soon, the only sound was the thrumming of the engines.

"See anything?" Connor asked.

Roshni peered into the murk. "Not yet," she said.

Connor took them deeper.

Roshni frowned at the sonar screen. "Still nothing."

"That's weird," Connor said. "I can't see any creatures at all down here. Not even a shrimp!"

The cabin suddenly became much darker. Something was blotting out all the light.

"Look!" Roshni pointed up. "Is that the whale pod?"

High above them passed a huge shadow.

"Could be," Connor said. "Let's take a look."

But as they drew close, Connor soon saw it wasn't the whales at all.

Hanging over them was an enormous cloud of bright red algae. It made the sea look like tomato soup. The algae covered the water for what looked like miles in every direction.

They surfaced in the middle of the stuff. Red liquid slid down the windows.

"It's like the surface of Mars," Roshni whispered in amazement.

"And about as much good for life," Connor said. "That's a red tide. Also known as an algal bloom."

Connor knew that this kind of algae was bad for marine life because it released poisons into the water. There was no sense in blaming the algae though. They fed on farm fertilizer that had been washed out to sea and grew so fast because climate change had warmed the oceans.

Human beings had caused this mess.

"No point looking for the whales here." He sighed. "They feed off these little critters called krill. Guess what a red tide does to krill?"

"Kills them?" Roshni guessed.

Connor nodded. "Let's keep moving."

He fired the engines. The Beagle churned

up the water and they plunged below the surface again. Connor was glad to leave that ugly red soup behind.

As they moved out of the algal bloom's shadow, the water began to clear. Little gleaming fish zipped past. Then came a pulsing jellyfish with tentacles like streamers. Connor smiled. This was more like it!

He steered them down toward the seabed. Roshni switched on the outside lights and gasped.

The beams lit up a wonderland of life. Before them lay brightly colored kelp beds, clumps of coral like heaps of treasure, and schools of glittering fish.

As they approached a bulging rock, it suddenly moved! The rock changed color and reached out with its striped tentacles. It snatched up a crab.

Roshni gave a yelp of surprise, then a delighted laugh. "It's an octopus!"

"A mimic octopus, and it's a beauty," said Connor. "They're camouflage experts."

"I noticed." Roshni grinned. "Hey, is that a shark? It looks like an alien."

Off in the distance, a pale gray shape was gliding along silently, looking for prey.

Its strange head was T-shaped, with eyes at the ends.

"Yep," said Connor. "A hammerhead."

They steered the Beagle carefully around the rocks and reefs, still searching for the whales. There was no sign. Once a hidden manta ray rose up from the seabed, sending clouds of sand everywhere. But there were still no whales.

"Maybe there's something on the sub that can help us," Roshni said, looking around. "Turbo boost..." She read out the labels under the buttons. "Grabbing arm... Hey, what about this sound scanner?"

"Go for it," Connor said.

Roshni pressed a switch. The cabin suddenly filled with the noises made by the different sea creatures outside. Crabs scuttled and clicked. A hammerhead shark thrashed its tail.

Then, from the dim distance, came an eerie, echoing sound. Connor froze. "Listen! That's them!"

They both held their breath. For almost a whole minute, there was only silence. Then they both heard it again, loud and clear.

Connor thought there was no other sound on Earth like the song of a humpback whale—a soaring, shivering, lonely call that somehow seemed to come from the far-off stars. His skin tingled.

"Wow," Roshni breathed.

"I know, right?" Connor pointed forward.

"They're definitely in that direction."

"Let's see if we can find them with the sonar!" Roshni said.

She pressed a button. Sure enough, the pod of whales popped up on the screen! They were swimming together over an underwater valley.

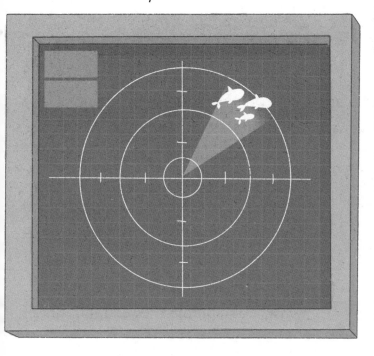

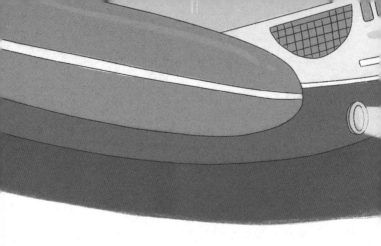

"We need to follow them!" Connor said.

Roshni's fingers danced over the controls. With a loud ping, a glowing green arrow appeared on the dashboard, pointing the way to the whales.

"Full speed ahead, Captain Connor!" she yelled.

"Aye, aye!" Connor growled and slammed the engines up to maximum thrust. They were flung back in their seats as the Beagle roared through the ocean like a torpedo.

It wasn't long before they caught sight of

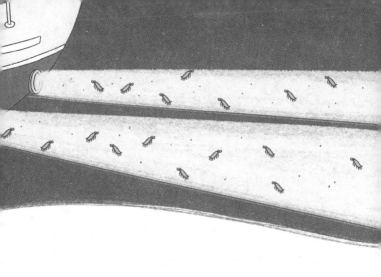

the same deep valley they'd seen with the sonar. Tiny creatures with lots of legs were swimming through the sub's headlights.

Krill!

Connor slowed the engines down. They had to be close.

Any moment now...

"There they are!" he said in an awed whisper.

The humpback whales were coming into view. One after another, their immense shapes emerged from the cloudy depths.

Connor looked on, his heart pounding, as their mighty tails beat a path through the ocean. How could something so enormous be so graceful?

"I hope the other Secret Explorers are watching right now," he said, "because this is the most awesome thing I've ever seen!"

Chapter Three
MAKE SOME NOISE

Now that he could see the humpback whales clearly, Connor was worried. They needed help, but what kind? He didn't like to think of these beautiful creatures being in danger.

"Can we get closer?" Roshni asked excitedly.

"Sure," Connor replied. "But not too close. We don't want to spook them."

He turned the engines down until they were coasting quietly through the water. As they drew closer to the pod, more and more whales emerged from the murk. He could clearly see the knobbly bumps on their heads and their wise little eyes.

Roshni's own eyes widened and she gasped. "Look, they've got *babies*!"

Connor looked where she was pointing. Sure enough, among the large whales were some little ones. They were only a few yards long, and each was swimming close to an adult whale. Those had to be their mothers.

"Calves," Connor said.

"Huh? Where?"

"That's what you call a baby whale. This mission just got even more important, Roshni."

Roshni nodded, her face serious. "We've got to protect these guys. So what's the danger? Predators?"

"I can't tell yet," Connor said. "But I know one thing. These whales give birth in Pacific waters, where it's warm. So now they must be migrating south to Antarctica. The water there is cold, but it's full of krill for them to eat."

The Beagle, which had been quiet until now, let out a sudden *BEEP!* Red lights flashed on the console.

Connor and Roshni stared at it.

Connor asked "What's up, Beagle? Did I get something wrong?"

BEEP! the Beagle repeated.

"Wait." Roshni held up a hand. "You said the whales were swimming south. But the sun's right in front of us right now. And the whales are swimming toward it. And it's nearly sunset, and the sun sets in the west. So that means..."

BLOO-BOOPOP, jabbered the Beagle encouragingly. It sounded like "keep talking."

"...the whales are swimming west, not south!" Roshni exclaimed.

Connor sat bolt upright in his seat. "You're right. They're swimming toward Australia, not Antarctica. The pod of whales is off course!"

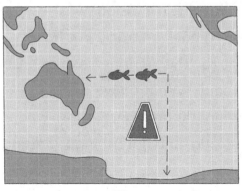

The Beagle made a triumphant *DING!* noise like someone ringing a bell.

"But how could the whales have gone the wrong way?" Roshni said. "They use the same migration route every year, don't they?"

Connor thought he knew what had happened. "Remember that red tide we saw? Maybe the whales didn't want to swim through that stuff. They might have gotten lost trying to avoid it."

They both looked out at the whales, who were all swimming powerfully in the wrong direction. Connor and Roshni understood now what their mission was—to get the whale pod back on track. But how?

"You're the marine expert, Connor," Roshni said. "What do we do?"

Connor thought hard. Those whales were huge, strong, and determined. Getting them

to change course wouldn't be easy. He tried to remember how other people had helped whales in the past.

"I read about a whale that was trapped in a harbor," he said. "It didn't know which way to go. Whales don't like loud sounds, so people banged on pipes and all kinds of other things to drive her in the right direction, so she could swim away to safety."

Roshni asked, "Could we do the same?"

"It's worth a try!" Connor grinned as an idea came to him. "Hey, remember when Kiki got us all to do karaoke in the Exploration Station that time?"

Roshni rolled her eyes. "How could I forget?"

Connor leaned over the console. "Hey, Beagle? Can you fire up your speakers and microphone, please?"

A panel popped open and a microphone slid out.

Connor pulled open the supplies compartment. "Grab anything you can make a noise with."

Moments later, they were armed with a metal First Aid kit, some screw drivers and wrenches, a piece of copper tubing, and a safety helmet. They were ready to make the most horrendous racket they could.

They needed to nudge the whales south, so Connor steered the Beagle around the pod to the north. That way, when all the humpback whales swam away from the  noise, they'd be heading in the right direction.

"Ready?" Connor said. "And a one, two, three, four..."

BANG! CRASH! CLANG! SKADOING!

The Beagle's cockpit rang with the din. Connor and Roshni made as much noise as they could, battering the helmet with the copper tube and clashing the tools together. The speakers broadcast the dreadful sounds into the sea all around.

One of the whales twitched a fin, but that was all.

"We need more noise!" Connor yelled. "Beagle, give me a beat!"

Instantly, the Beagle boomed out a rhythm. Roshni joined in, making beatbox noises. Connor grabbed the microphone and belted out a rap, making up the lyrics as he went along:

"It's time for you to move along! It's time for you to bail, whale!

You got another place to be! Come on and move your tail, whale!

You know you're going way too slow, so please don't be a snail, whale!

It's time for your migration and we need you not to fail, whale!"

Slowly but surely, the whales began to turn.

"It's working!" Connor cried out.

"I'm not surprised," Roshni joked. "That has to be the worst rapping I've ever heard in my life. I think I cringed my way into a parallel universe!"

They followed the pod to make sure the whales were really on the right course. Connor let himself relax a little. The whales would be okay now. He could just sit back and watch them swim. Now that he had the time to count them, he did—there were eighteen adults and three calves.

Roshni pointed. "That one's swimming up to the surface. Is it okay?"

"It's fine!" Connor told her. "Whales aren't fish. They're mammals, like us, so they breathe air, not water. To do that, they go up to the surface every few minutes."

"So how do they breathe, then?" Roshni asked.

"Through blowholes on the tops of their heads," Connor explained. "They're like big nostrils."

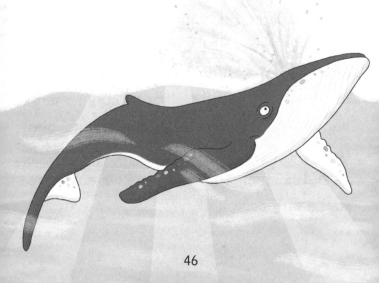

Roshni took a breath, held it as long as she could, and then gasped for air. "I don't think I'd make a very good whale," she wheezed.

Connor chuckled. "An adult humpback whale can last up to *forty-five minutes* between breaths. Can you imagine?"

"That's incredible," Roshni said. "Listen, they're singing again!"

The haunting sound of whale song rippled through the water. Roshni listened to it for a moment, her face frozen in wonder. Then she looked thoughtful, pressed some buttons on the Beagle's console and opened an instrument panel.

"What are you doing?" Connor asked.

"Recording the whale song," Roshni replied. "It's so beautiful, I want to listen to it when we're back on land."

Connor laughed. "Okay, I admit it. They're better singers than I am!"

Roshni glanced from her recording equipment over to the sonar screen. "Hey, look. There's a whole bunch of signals up on the surface, moving around. Could it be another pod of whales?"

Connor frowned. "Maybe. We'd better go up and have a look."

He gunned the engines and steered the Beagle to the surface. When they bobbed up, Connor was startled. They were much closer to Australia than he'd realized. He could clearly see land on the horizon—and the reason for the sonar signals...

Boats!

There were dozens of them on the water. Some had sails, some had motors, and they were all zipping along.

Roshni said, "The whales are going to need to come up for air, aren't they? What if they come up under those boats?"

"It would be very bad news," said Connor seriously. "We need to get the pod safely past these boats. Roshni, our mission's not over yet!"

Chapter Four
BOATS AHOY!

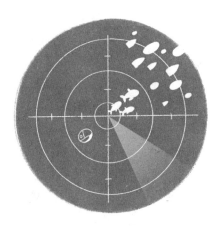

The sonar screen showed more dots than Connor and Roshni could count. Every single one was a boat—and they were heading right into the whales' path.

"So many boats! Is it a race or something?" Roshni asked, looking worried.

"It's just regular marine traffic," said Connor. "People going out fishing and having fun. And not one of them knows a pod of whales is about to swim right under their hulls!"

"We've got to warn them," Roshni said. "I'll try to contact one of the boats on the radio."

She flicked a switch on the Beagle's communications equipment. But the Beagle switched it back off again, with a warning *BUZZ*.

"Looks like the Beagle isn't happy about that," Connor said. "Wonder why?"

Roshni snapped her fingers. "Of course. We're the Secret Explorers—and we're supposed to stay secret! If we call those boats on our radio, they'll want to know who we are and what we're doing here."

"Maybe there's another way." Connor thought hard. "Beagle, can you zoom in on that yacht over there?"

The yacht was floating not far from where the Beagle bobbed on the surface. A close-up appeared on the screen, showing white sails and a sleek hull. The name *Enchantress* was written down the yacht's side.

On the deck was a boy about their age. He was wearing swim trunks and watching something intently. Had he spotted the Beagle? No—he was looking at a school of flying fish! They came leaping out of the water in glittering arcs. Their bodies flashed silver in the warm evening sunlight.

Connor was glad to see someone else who was interested in the ocean. "Maybe that boy can help," he said.

Connor submerged the Beagle just below the water. He and Roshni took the wet suits out of the storage cupboard and put them on, along with masks, oxygen tanks, and flippers.

Then he opened up a hatch in the floor, revealing water beneath. Connor climbed down first, lowering himself into the ocean. Roshni followed behind him. They swam away from the Beagle toward the pale hull of the *Enchantress*.

Connor surfaced right alongside the yacht. The boy was still watching the ocean, and he gave a surprised yelp as Connor and then Roshni appeared.

Connor waved up to him. "Hey! Mind if we come aboard?"

The boy gave them a wide grin. "Yeah, no worries!"

Roshni reached up and the boy helped her climb onto the deck, then did the same for Connor.

"I'm Jack," he said. "I've come out with my parents to do a bit of whale watching. But there are no whales so far today."

"Whales are exactly why we're here!" Connor said. "There's a pod of humpback whales swimming this way, but all these fast boats could be dangerous for them."

"No way!" Jack exclaimed.

Connor said, "There's still time to save them. We just need to clear all these boats out of their path. Can you signal to them to move?"

"You just watch me, mate," Jack said excitedly. "I'll get my parents to call the coastguard. When you hear the horn means we're on the move!" He ran o the cabin door and shouted, "Mor It's an emergency!"

"We'd better get out of here," Roshni whispered to Connor.

Connor nodded. "Thanks a million, Jack! Good luck!"

Before Jack's parents could appear, Connor and Roshni flipped backward off the deck and plunged into the water. They swam back to the Beagle as fast as they could. Soon they were climbing back up through the hatch, peeling off their wet suits and turning back to the controls.

Connor checked the sonar. His heart pounded. The whales were swimming right under the boats! If one of them surfaced now, it would mean disaster.

"Come on, Jack," he muttered. "Don't let us down..."

A long horn-blast rang out across the water.

"There's the signal!" Roshni cried.

Connor checked the periscope.

"The boats are moving. They're all heading back toward the shore!"

Roshni clapped her hands. "Jack's done it!"

Connor brought the Beagle back to the surface so they could watch what was happening. Sure enough, the boats were all sailing out of the whales' path. He caught a glimpse of Jack standing on the deck of the *Enchantress*, looking at the water again. Suddenly, a humpback whale came up to the surface and blew!

A great cheer went up from Jack and the other people watching from the boats. Another whale came up, and then another. Connor smiled to himself. The pod was safe!

"Let's get back to the whales," he said. "I want to make sure they're all okay."

He submerged the Beagle once more. But as they closed in on the whales, Connor saw to his dismay that the pod was off course again. Instead of heading south, the whales were now swimming east!

"The boats must have upset them so much they turned all the way around," he said with a groan. "We're right back where we started!"

"Actually, I think it's worse," Roshni said in a hollow voice.

"What? How?" Connor asked.

Roshni pointed. "How many calves did the whales have before?"

"Three," said Connor.

All eighteen of the adult whales were still there, swimming ahead. But Connor could only see two calves.

"They've lost one!" he said. "But if all the mothers are still here..."

"... then wherever that poor calf is, it's all alone," Roshni finished. "Connor, we've got to find it!"

Chapter Five
DEEP, DARK WATERS

The rest of the pod was already moving on. Connor wished he could call out to them. *Turn around! You've left a calf behind!*

"We'll have to backtrack," he said. "Maybe the calf is swimming behind the rest of the pod."

He steered the Beagle back the way they had come. Meanwhile, Roshni carefully watched the sonar screen for any sign of the lost calf. Connor kept the Beagle just under the water's surface, so they could use the periscope. The calf might come up to breathe, and then they'd spot it.

"Poor little thing," Roshni murmured. "Don't worry, baby whale. We're coming to find you."

Connor said, "It may be a baby, but it's about 20 feet long! We ought to see it soon."

Roshni bent over the sonar screen. Connor peered out through the Beagle's windows. He saw darting fish and scraps of seaweed tumbling past, but no whale calf. To make matters worse, the sun was setting and the sea was growing darker. Soon it would be too dark to see without lights.

Suddenly, the Beagle pitched sideways and a horrific sound of scraping metal ripped through the cabin. Then came a sharp snapping noise. Something fell through the water past the window, trailing bubbles. The Beagle let out a babble of panicked bleeps. Roshni yelled and looked up from the screen. "What happened?"

"We've hit something!" Connor grabbed the controls and brought the Beagle down, away from the surface. He smacked his forehead with his palm. "I was looking out of

the window, you were checking the sonar—
and neither of us was steering! Sorry, Beagle."

The Beagle made a mournful noise, like
a whining dog. Connor felt terrible.

He looked up at the hull of the boat
they'd clipped, dreading what he might see.
To his relief, it wasn't holed. That could have
been a total disaster. Imagine sinking a boat
and losing a whale calf...

"I think we might be okay," he said.
"We took a nasty knock, but nothing's
broken, right?"

Roshni winced and showed him the sonar screen. It was completely blank.

With growing alarm, Connor checked the rest of the Beagle's instruments. The screens had gone dark on a whole row of panels.

"We've lost all our navigation systems," he said. "But how?"

Roshni said, "Remember that snapping noise? And the thing that fell past the window? I think that was the navigation module. It must have broken off completely when we hit the boat."

Connor felt cold horror creeping through his whole body. Without the Beagle's special navigation module, they couldn't work the sonar or the satnav system. He was counting on that to find the missing calf. And even if they found the calf without it, how on earth would they find the rest of the pod?

"We've got to get it back!" he said.

He tilted the Beagle's nose until it was pointing downward, then fired the engines. They churned up the water and the Beagle shot down into the darkness. The controls vibrated in Connor's hands, but he held the sub steady. *No more collisions*, he promised himself.

"I can see it!" cried Roshni.

Sure enough, the broken-off navigation module was ahead of them, turning over and over as it fell through the water. It looked like half a soccer ball, with wires and cables hanging out from it. Connor winced as he remembered seeing it attached to the top of the cockpit. He hoped they'd be able to reattach it.

The next moment it vanished from sight, swallowed up in the darkness. The water outside the sub was as black as the bottom of a well.

The Beagle made a serious-sounding **BLEEEEP**. Connor knew that the deeper they dived, the higher the water pressure. Now it would be closing on the Beagle like a clenching fist. At the same time, it was getting colder and colder.

Connor shivered.

He checked the depth gauge and saw they were nearly at the bottom of the ocean. Connor slowed the Beagle to a stop and looked around.

"Shouldn't we turn on the headlights?" asked Roshni.

"Not yet," Connor said. "Look."

Strange lights were glowing in the darkness. Roshni stared at them. "What are they?"

"That one there is an Atolla jellyfish," Connor said, pointing out a blue flashing light. "It flashes when it's under attack. And that steady glow? That's an angler fish. The light lures smaller fish in, so it can eat them."

"I've never seen anything like it," Roshni said.

Connor switched the headlights on and lit up the angler fish's whole body. Beneath the pretty light was a ghoulish face and a mouth full of pointed teeth! Roshni shuddered.

"The light's called bioluminescence," Connor explained. "It's created by a chemical reaction."

"Wow!" Roshni glanced up at a billowy shape that was drifting by overhead. "What's that one?"

Connor wasn't sure what the pale creature might be. "Some kind of jellyfish, I think. It's coming this way."

Roshni's face fell. "Oh, dear. I think this is a member of the species *plasticus baggus*."

Connor grimaced in disgust. "Yeah," he said. The mysterious "jellyfish" was nothing but a supermarket plastic bag, swept along by the undersea currents. It sickened him to think of plastic pollution down here among these wonderful ocean creatures.

Roshni said, "I'll swim out and get it."

She went to put her wet suit back on, but Connor quickly stopped her. "No!"

"What's wrong?"

Connor pointed out the water pressure gauge. "We can't go out there. At this depth, the pressure would crush us!"

But they couldn't just leave the plastic bag on the ocean floor. They began exploring the Beagle's cockpit, in the hope of finding something that might help.

"Aha!" Connor said. "The grabber arm! We can use that!"

He found the switch and turned it on. A long robotic arm slid out from the Beagle's underside. Connor moved it back and forth and tested the grabber.

"How is it?" Roshni asked.

"Easier to use than the claw machines at the arcade," Connor joked.

As the plastic bag drifted back in their direction, Connor used the robotic arm to quickly snatch it up. The Beagle helpfully opened up a storage compartment and Connor stowed the bag inside.

"Scientists use arms just like this on research subs," he told Roshni. "They can take samples from the seabed or recover items from sunken ships!"

"And we can use it to get the navigation module back!" Roshni burst out.

"Brilliant idea," Connor said. "But... where is it?"

In the excitement of seeing the luminous sea creatures, they'd lost track of the module. Now they couldn't see it anywhere.

Connor's stomach tightened into a knot. If they didn't find the module it would pollute the water, just like the plastic bag.

"We've got to find it," Connor said. "If we don't, we'll never find the calf and the rest of the whale pod!"

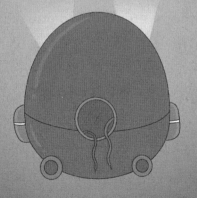

Chapter Six

UNDER PRESSURE

Connor adjusted the Beagle's headlights until they were pointing down at the seabed. Then he set the Beagle so it would move automatically in a circle around where the module had fallen. That way, they would have the best chance of spotting it.

"Do you see it yet?" he asked Roshni.

"Not yet," she said.

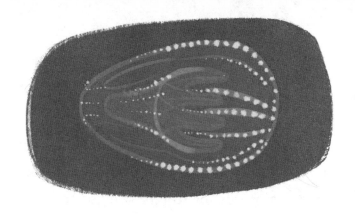

"Come on," Connor said through gritted teeth. "Where is it?"

Above them, in the darkness, rainbow light glimmered.

Roshni gasped. "What's that?"

Connor recognized it at once. "It's a real jellyfish this time! It's called a comb jelly. Another bioluminescent species."

"It's pretty!" said Roshni. "It looks like it's covered in tiny stars."

The jellyfish was about 18 inches long. It floated above their heads, bright twinkles sparkling on its transparent body.

"Why do the creatures down here glow?" Roshni asked.

"Lots of reasons," Connor said. "Scientists think it might be a way to communicate with other creatures, or to lure prey so they can catch it. Or they might be trying to scare away rivals."

"But there aren't any other creatures here," Roshni said thoughtfully. "Unless..."

She grabbed the headlight control and swiveled the beams of light in the direction the comb jelly had come from.

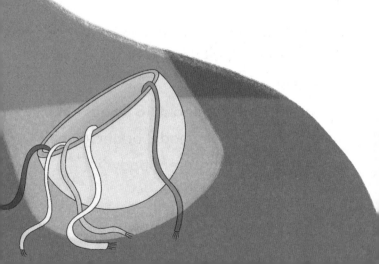

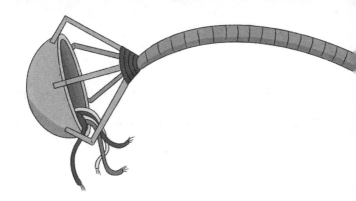

There, wedged in an outcrop of undersea rock, was the missing navigation module!

"Maybe the jelly thought the module was another creature!" Connor exclaimed.

"Thanks, little guy," Roshni called back at the departing jelly.

Connor extended the robotic arm, took hold of the navigation module and stowed it safely in the storage compartment. The Beagle let out a long beep that sounded a lot like "Phew!"

Connor felt relieved, too. Now they could get back to their mission! He just hoped it wasn't too late for the lost whale calf.

He brought the Beagle back up to the surface. Then he lowered himself through the hatch and climbed up the outside of the sub and onto the roof. Roshni used the robotic arm to lift the navigation module back into place. Connor did his best to reconnect all the wires and cables, but engineering wasn't his specialty subject. Sparks shot out, and the Beagle made an unhappy **EEP!**

Connor climbed back inside the cabin. "I don't think we can do this by ourselves. We'd better call the others," he told Roshni.

Roshni switched on the communications panel. "Beagle calling Exploration Station! We need help!"

An image of the Exploration Station appeared on the screen, showing all the other Secret Explorers at their computers. They waved.

"We've all been watching your mission on our monitors!" Leah said.

"Yeah!" said Cheng with a grin. "You're doing brilliantly!"

"Do you think the whales are going to be okay?" Tamiko asked nervously.

"I'm sure we can still help them," Connor assured her. "But we need to fix the Beagle. And quick. Kiki, you're the Engineering Explorer. Can you talk us through the repairs?"

"Show me the damage," Kiki said.

Connor held the broken module up to the screen.

Kiki sucked air through her teeth. "Yeesh! You two really did a number on that module, didn't you? I couldn't fix that without my special workbench, guys. I'm sorry."

"Thanks anyway, Kiki," Connor said. "We'll figure something out."

"Good luck! We're all rooting for you here," said Gustavo.

The other Secret Explorers waved goodbye. Connor and Roshni waved, too, and shut the communicator off. The two of them shared a worried glance.

"So what are we supposed to do now?" Roshni asked.

Connor pressed his knuckles to his forehead and thought as hard as he could. The lost calf was nowhere to be seen. Nor was the rest of the pod. Worse still, the sun had almost vanished behind the western horizon. Without either the sun or the navigation module to help them, they couldn't tell which way was south. So they couldn't help the whales get back on the right course.

Maybe I should try thinking like a whale, he thought to himself.

How did whales find their way around their underwater world? They used sonar, but they didn't have electric equipment. They made their own sound waves and bounced them off objects. Dolphins did it, too, and it was how bats navigated through the night sky.

Maybe sound was the answer...

"I wonder if we could use sound to find the missing calf," he said.

"I'm not sure," Roshni said. "You don't want to scare the calf away with your terrible rapping, do you?"

Connor sighed. "Yeah. It was a silly idea. If I could sing like a whale, maybe things would be different..."

He froze. An idea had just lit up like a light bulb inside his mind.

"Why didn't I think of this before? We *can* sing like a whale!" he yelled. "Roshni, you're a genius!"

Roshni looked puzzled. "I am? Thanks, I guess! But what did I do?"

Connor used the Beagle's console to find the sound file Roshni had made earlier. "You recorded the whale song, remember? We can play it through the speakers!"

Roshni's face brightened. "Will that bring the lost calf over to us?"

"I don't know, but I really hope so," Connor said. "Because I think it's our last chance!"

Chapter Seven
WHALE SONG

Roshni switched the microphone and speakers back on. Connor clicked the "PLAY" button and the whale song began. It swelled out from the sub, echoing far into the dark and lonely depths.

They looked around hopefully. Connor felt a rush of excitement as he saw something swimming toward them, about the right size to be the calf. But then it turned sideways to pass them, and he saw the long spike protruding from its nose. It was a swordfish! Any other time, he'd have been overjoyed to see it.

The whale song stopped. He quickly clicked the "PLAY" button again.

Connor chewed his lip anxiously as they peered into the shadows. But there was nothing but swirling sediment and tiny fish. The whale song ended again. He crossed his fingers for luck and played it one more time.

Then, out of nowhere, a shape appeared. A humpbacked shape 20 feet long and swimming curiously toward them...

Connor was about to yell, "It's the calf!" But, just in time, he remembered the microphone was still on! He tapped Roshni's shoulder and put his finger to his lips. Her eyes widened as she saw it.

Connor tried to imagine what the calf was thinking. What could this strange thing be, which sounded like a whale but wasn't one and was all lit up with bright and shiny lights?

The calf swam around the Beagle. Roshni put her hand up to the window pane, just as

the calf pressed against it.

"It's like I'm touching it!" she whispered.

Connor watched the calf in amazement. It turned around to face him. For one instant he looked right into its eye, and a thrill went through his whole body. He had never been this close to such an astonishing creature.

The calf gazed at Connor, and Connor looked back at it. It didn't look afraid, and he was deeply glad of that. Then, without warning, it rolled all the way over.

"What's it doing?" Roshni asked.

The calf lashed its tail, looked at them, and rolled over again. Strange clicking noises came from it. Connor recognized the funny noises as whale language.

"It's trying to play with us!" he said, and laughed in delight. "The calf knows the Beagle is a friend."

The Beagle made a joyful **SQUEAK** through its console. The calf heard it through the speakers and let loose a series of happy clicks in response.

Then, from somewhere close by, more whale song came booming through the water.

"Could that be the mother whale, calling for her calf?" asked Roshni.

"It's not just one whale," Connor replied. "Look at that!"

Suddenly, enormous whales loomed all around them!

The entire pod had answered their call. A chorus of whale song greeted the lost calf, welcoming it back. The Beagle seemed very tiny next to these magnificent creatures.

Roshni gave Connor a hug. "I'm glad you got to see this," she said. "I know how much you love the oceans."

He grinned and hugged her back. "Look at them! They're not scared of us at all.

I think... maybe they understand what we've been trying to do."

They watched the whales swim around them for a moment and listened to their uncanny song.

Roshni pointed. "Connor, look!" The calf and its mother had found one another again. They were swimming close together, side by side. Humpback whales can't smile, but Connor was sure those two would if they could.

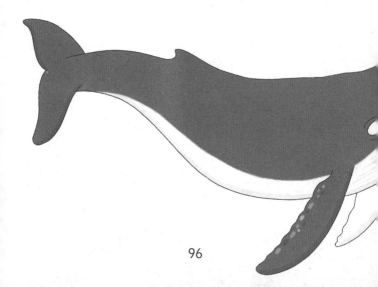

They certainly looked happy to be reunited.

He and Roshni cheered and high-fived one another.

"We still need to get the pod back on its correct migration course," Connor said.

Roshni nodded. "Which means heading south."

"But how? The sun's gone down, and we couldn't fix the navigation module."

Connor looked out at the pod and hoped he hadn't let the whales down after all.

Roshni pondered for a moment.

"It might not matter that the sun's gone down. Remember what I said about the comb jelly?"

Connor thought back. "You said its body looked like it was covered in stars."

"Right! And that's given me an idea. The sun might be down, but the stars will be out, won't they? If I can find the right constellations, I can navigate by the stars!"

"Of course!" Connor said.

"Sailors have used stars to find their way for thousands of years," Roshni said.

"But you're the Space Explorer – I thought you wanted to be an astronaut, not a sailor?" Connor joked.

"Where do you think the word 'astronaut' comes from?" Roshni said with a grin." *Astron* means star, and *nautes* means sailor. Astronauts are literally star sailors!"

Connor brought the Beagle up to the surface. The night sky was filled with stars. Roshni looked up and searched the sky.

"There!" she cried out, pointing to a group of four stars. "Do you see it, Connor? The Southern Cross!"

"Yeah," Connor said. Those stars were so bright, he could hardly have missed them. They stood out like jewels on a black cloth.

Roshni frowned in concentration. "Here's what you do. Draw an imaginary line from the top star through to the bottom. Then keep the line going for four and a half times that length."

"Got it," Connor said, picturing the line in his mind.

"Great! Now drop another line straight down from the end of the first line. Where it hits the horizon marks due south!"

Connor could hardly believe it. "It's really that easy?"

Roshni laughed. "It is when you know how!"

Connor set the whale song playing again, while Roshni steered the Beagle south. With any luck, the whales would follow the song.

Connor didn't need to worry. The whales seemed to know what they were doing. They followed along behind the sub, answering the whale song he was playing with a song of their own.

"Funny to think that we dove deep under the sea, but the answer was in the stars all along," Roshni said happily.

"I guess now we know why the Space Explorer got sent on an underwater mission," Connor said with a grin. "I'm really glad you're here, Roshni!"

Chapter Eight
HEADING HOME

The farther south they went, the colder the waters became. Connor knew they must be well on their way to Antarctica.

After the Beagle had guided the pod of whales south for a while, all at once they suddenly began to swim much faster. A new, excited mood seemed to have come over them. They swam right past the Beagle and kept going.

"What's happening? Are the whales okay?" asked Roshni.

"They're fine, I think," Connor replied. "They must recognize where they are. They're back on their migration route!"

One by one, the whales overtook them. Last of all came the mother whale and the calf they'd rescued, who was swimming right beside her. The mother whale broke away from the others and began swimming up to the surface.

Roshni and Connor traded glances. Without saying a word, Connor guided the Beagle after her. He kept the sub a safe distance away.

They reached the surface first and looked out over the glittering dark waters.

"What's she doing?" Roshni asked.

"Just watch," Connor whispered.

The whale launched herself out of the water. Time seemed to slow down as her enormous body rose, turned and fell. She came crashing down onto her back, sending foam and water up

in a massive burst. The Beagle rocked around crazily.

Moments later, the little calf flung itself out of the water, copying what its mother had done. It made a much smaller splash, but Connor and Roshni still clapped and cheered!

One by one, the other whales rose, too. They blew jets of spray from their blowholes, then dived back down again.

"I think they're saying goodbye," Roshni said.

Connor nodded. "Goodbye," he called out to them. "I'll never forget this."

The last of the whales vanished below the surf. The flukes that flared out at the end of its huge tail flicked for a moment, like a vast waving hand. Then it was gone.

"They'll be okay from here, right?" Roshni asked.

"More than okay," Connor replied. "They'll find their way to the Antarctic just fine. They don't need our help anymore."

With a soft **PING**, the "START" button on the Beagle's dashboard lit up. Now it read "HOME." Connor and Roshni breathed a sigh of relief. "Mission accomplished," Roshni said. "Let's go!"

Connor pushed the button.

The Beagle shuddered and trembled, as if it were going through a car wash. The engines behind them gave a deafening roar. Suddenly, like they were being shot from a massive rubber band, the Beagle rushed forward at mindboggling speed. They were whizzing through a tunnel of dazzling white light.

Around them, the Beagle's cockpit began to change. The dashboard sank back into the floor, the glass bubble slid backward and vanished, the padded seats deflated like an air bed, all the compartments and equipment folded away like a magic trick, and four

rather wobbly-looking wheels appeared on the corners. Once more, the Beagle was nothing but a shabby old go-kart... with a lot of secrets.

The white light faded away. The Beagle was standing on its platform in the middle of the Exploration Station. Feeling a little dizzy, Connor and Roshni climbed out of the seats.

All the other Secret Explorers jumped up from their computer chairs and came sprinting over. They gathered excitedly around Connor and Roshni.

"That was amazing!" Cheng said. "All those undersea rock formations!"

"And the different kinds of seaweed!" Leah said.

"What was it like when the whale breached?" asked Gustavo.

"You guys did an amazing job," Ollie said. "I'm so glad the whales are safe."

Connor and Roshni sat on the big padded sofas, had some cold drinks, and talked all about their mission. All the Secret Explorers agreed it had been a spectacular success.

"Hey, Kiki," Connor said, "do you think you can fix the damage to the Beagle? Whoever takes it out on the next mission is going to need that navigation module."

"No problem!" Kiki grinned. "The Beagle is always getting into scrapes. I'll patch it right up."

Leah went and opened the display cabinets. "Did you bring anything back for the collection?"

Connor took a thumb drive out of his pocket. He'd copied the whale song recording on to it earlier.

"You're going to want to listen to this."

He played the sound file through the Exploration Station speakers.

When the Secret Explorers heard the strange sounds echoing around the room, their faces filled with awe. No one said a word. They all looked up at the domed ceiling, where the map of the night sky was, and listened to the unearthly music of the whales.

Afterward, Connor put the thumb drive in the display case between a piece of black volcanic glass that Cheng had collected and a bonsai tree that Leah had brought from Japan.

It was time to go home. "Bye, Roshni," Connor said. "Bye, everyone! See you on the next mission!"

Everyone waved and called out their goodbyes. Connor headed over to the glowing door he'd come in by, and stepped back through it.

A raging wind whipped through his hair and ruffled his clothes. White light roared up around him and faded away just as quickly. Seconds later, he found himself standing in his kitchen.

He glanced back over his shoulder. The pantry was just a pantry. There were cereal boxes, cans of beans, a bag of potatoes—nothing at all out of the ordinary. Nothing to show that anything exciting had ever happened here.

Connor could almost believe that he'd dreamed the whole adventure. But he knew he hadn't. No time at all had passed back here at home, but he'd been gone for several hours, and now he was hungry.

He reached up and took a granola bar from the shelf and headed outside to eat it. He crouched down beside the pond, unwrapped the bar, and took a bite.

Down in the pond, the toad tadpoles were peacefully swimming in their shoals. They looked like they were enjoying the clear water.

Connor grinned to see them. Swimming together like that, they reminded him of the pod of whales. He'd keep on looking out for the tadpoles, just as he had for the pod. And though he couldn't just scoop the red tide out of the ocean as easily as he'd scooped the green algae out of his own little pond, he could still do his part to help keep the seas clean.

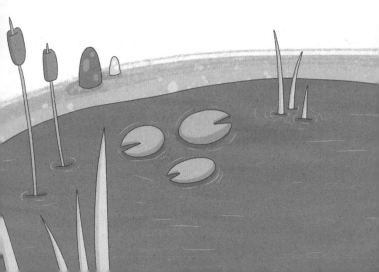

Connor loved being a Secret Explorer. This mission had been one of the best yet. And he couldn't wait to go on the next one!

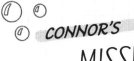

CONNOR'S
MISSION NOTES

THE HUMPBACK WHALE

* **Latin name**: *Megaptera novaeangliae*

* **Animal type**: Mammals—they breathe air, have warm blood, and give birth to live young

* **Location**: Worldwide, but usually nearer coasts

* **Length**: Up to 56 ft (17 m)

* **Weight**: 37 tons (34 metric tons)—heavier than five African elephants!

In the southern oceans, humpback feed mainly on Antarctic krill.

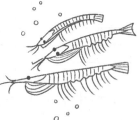

Each whale has a unique pattern on the underside of its tail.

The pectoral flippers of the humpback are one-third of its body length—longer than those of other whales.

WHAT A TUNE!

Male humpbacks make sounds known as whale songs. These calls can be heard by whales many miles away and last for up to 30 minutes. Scientists think they might be a way to attract females, to protect their territory, or to communicate with each other.

BEHAVIOR

* Every year, most humpbacks migrate to warm waters to give birth to their young. They swim thousands of miles.

* Humpbacks live in groups called "pods," which include up to 15 whales.

* An adult humpback can hold its breath underwater for 45 minutes—but usually stays under for 10–15 minutes before coming up for air.

The humpback has a pair of huge nostrils on the top of its head. These are called blowholes, and they close when the whales dive underwater.

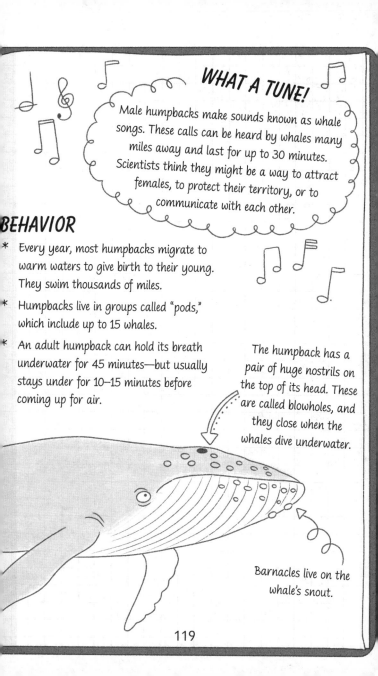

Barnacles live on the whale's snout.

OCEAN LIFE

Sunlit zone

* Top 650 ft (200 m) of the ocean.
* Lots of different animals live in this zone, including humpback whales.
* It is also home to tiny creatures called plankton, which includes baby crabs and fish eggs. They float around on the currents. Many sea creatures depend on plankton for food.

Twilight zone

* From 650 ft to 3,300 ft (200 m to 1, 000 m) below the surface.
* The little sunlight that reaches this zone gives it a faint blue glow. Fewer animals live here than in the sunlit zone.
* Some areas of this zone don't have much oxygen, so the only animals that can live here have special adaptations.

Midnight zone

* More than 3,300 ft (1,000 m) down, no light at all reaches this zone.
* It is up to 33,000 ft (10,000 m) deep in places.
* Some of the creatures that live here are bioluminescent—they create their own light. For example, the anglerfish has a lure on top of its head that glows in the dark to attract prey—a bit like a fishing pole.

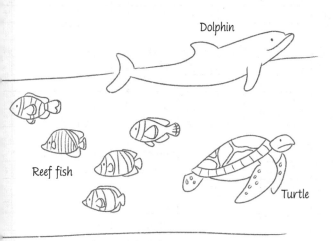
Dolphin

Reef fish

Turtle

Lantern fish

Comb jellyfish

Vampire squid

Anglerfish

Deep sea squid

Viperfish

OCEANS IN DANGER!

The Earth's climate is getting warmer—which is bad news for the oceans. Rising temperatures affect the life cycles of certain sea creatures, threatening their survival.

GLOBAL WARMING

Greenhouse gases, such as carbon dioxide and methane, build up in the atmosphere. This causes a greenhouse effect, as the gases stop heat from leaving the Earth's atmosphere—just like the glass windows that keep a greenhouse warm.

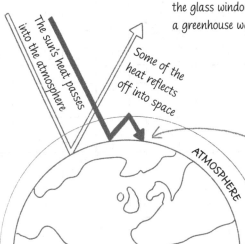

The sun's heat passes into the atmosphere

Some of the heat reflects off into space

Some of the heat is trapped in the atmosphere by greenhouse gases.

ATMOSPHERE

WHAT CAUSES IT?

* Burning fossil fuels such as coal, gas, and oil to generate electricity and power vehicles. When fossil fuels are burned, they release carbon dioxide into the atmosphere.

* Cutting down trees that absorb carbon dioxide. They are the world's best natural air filters!

* Cows' burping and farting releases lots of methane. In addition, forests are often cut down to clear land for them to graze.

THINGS THAT MAKE THE OCEAN SAD...

Warming seas and increased amounts of carbon dioxide and pollution in the water are destroying coral reefs. This leads to the loss of many fish and other animals.

Millions of tons of plastic end up in our oceans each year. Ocean animals can accidentally eat tiny bits of plastic in the water, or get caught in the garbage.

QUIZ

1. What is the name for a group of whales?

2. For how long can an adult humpback whale hold its breath underwater?

3. Which shark has a T-shaped head with eyes at the ends?

4. What do humpback whales eat?

5. What is a red tide made of?

6. Where would you find a humpback whale's blowholes?

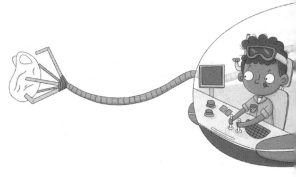

7   What do the Atolla jellyfish, the anglerfish, and the comb jelly all have in common?

8   What is a baby whale called?

FIND THE SEA DRAGONS!

Throughout the book we've hidden eight camouflaged sea dragons—can you find them?

They look like this!

Check your answers on page 129

GLOSSARY

ALGAE

a group of plant-like organisms, most of which live in water

ALGAL BLOOM

a rapid increase in the growth of algae

ASTRONAUT

a person who has been trained to travel into space

BARNACLE

a shelled sea creature that attaches itself tightly to rocks and other surfaces

BIOLUMINESCENCE

when a living organism produces its own light

CHARLES DARWIN

English naturalist who studied animals and plants

CONSTELLATION
a group of stars
that form
a pattern

FOSSIL FUELS
the remains of
organisms that died
millions of years ago
that can be burned
to release energy

GLOBAL WARMING
an increase in
global temperature
due to high
greenhouse
gas levels

GREENHOUSE GAS
a gas in the
atmosphere that
traps the sun's
warmth around
the planet, such
as carbon dioxide
and methane

HARBOR
a place on the
coast where
boats can dock

HORIZON
the line where
the sky seems to
meet the sea

KRILL
small shrimp-like
animal eaten by
many sea creatures,
including whales

MARINE BIOLOGIST
someone who
studies ocean life

MIGRATION
when animals make
a long, regular
journey from one
place to another

POD
a name for a
group of whales

POLLUTION
something harmful
that gets into
the air, a water
source, or the soil

SCHOOL
a group
of fish swimming
together

SONAR
a system that
locates things
underwater or
in the air using
sound echoes

SUBMARINE
a ship designed
to work underwater

TADPOLE
a young frog or toad

WATER PRESSURE
the amount of
pressure exerted
by water. Water
pressure increases
the deeper
you dive

WET SUIT
a close-fitting piece
of clothing worn
while diving

Quiz answers

1. Pod

2. 45 minutes

3. Hammerhead

4. Krill

5. Algae

6. On top of
   its head

7. They are all
   bioluminescent
   (give off their
   own light)

8. Calf

THE SECRET EXPLORERS AND THE COMET COLLISION

Chapter One
STARGAZING

Roshni attached her telescope to its stand. Excitement buzzed through her. "I really hope I see it tonight," she said to herself.

She was on the shore of Pangong Lake in India. The water seemed almost as still and quiet as the surface of the moon. Roshni's parents were talking in low voices over by the campfire. The vast Himalayan

Mountains loomed in the distance, their great dark shapes blotting out part of the sky. Overhead, thousands of stars shone like glittering dust.

It was chilly, but Roshni didn't mind. She wasn't scared of the dark, either. She loved it!

In fact, the less light there was, the better. You couldn't see the stars as well in a city, because of the streetlights. But out here, so far from the nearest town, the stars stood out in brilliant pinpoints. *This is the perfect place to stargaze*, thought Roshni.

She finished setting up her telescope and peered through the lens. It wasn't a toy—it was a real scientific instrument, and almost three feet long. Roshni was very proud of it. Down the side, she'd written her favorite saying: *The night hides a world, but reveals a universe*.

She carefully adjusted the telescope and a planet shone brightly against the dark.

"I can see you, Jupiter!" she whispered, and grinned. "Hi there, big guy."

It was June, the time of year when Jupiter's orbit brought it closest to Earth. Roshni had seen Jupiter before, but never this clearly. She could even make out its colored bands.

What Roshni really wanted to see was the enormous storm on Jupiter's surface. This was called the Great Red Spot. Roshni imagined that it would look like the eye of an angry giant! But she couldn't zoom in any farther.

She sighed. Her beloved telescope just wasn't powerful enough.

"I know!" she said. "My new lens!" Her parents had bought it for her to improve her telescope. Could it make Jupiter's image big enough to see the Great Red Spot?

She jumped up from the telescope, ran over to her little tent—and stopped in her tracks.

A compass symbol had appeared on her tent flap. It was glowing.

Roshni knew that symbol well. Pinned to her jacket was a badge in the exact same shape—the sign of the Secret Explorers!

Grinning to herself, Roshni scrambled through the tent flaps and into brilliant white light. Wind whistled through her hair and ruffled her jacket. She felt as if she were

plunging as fast as a meteor through the sky.

A couple of seconds later, the light faded. Roshni looked around. She was surrounded by the familiar black stone

136

walls of the Exploration Station, which gleamed like mirrors. A row of computer screens flickered.

"Roshni—here!" she yelled.

The only other person around was Tamiko, who was arranging some fossils in a display cabinet. "Hi!" Tamiko called and waved to her.

Roshni waved back. "Dinosaur bones?"

"Of course!" Tamiko said with a grin. She was the Dinosaur Explorer.

Roshni couldn't wait to find out why the Secret Explorers had been summoned this time. She jumped onto the huge, squishy sofa to watch the others arrive.

Overhead, on the domed ceiling, was an image of the Milky Way. On the floor was a huge map of the world. As the Secret Explorers came running through the glowing doorway, tiny lights flashed up from one country after another, showing where they were arriving from.

"Connor—here!" Connor waved at Roshni and Tamiko. He was the Marine Explorer and knew all about the oceans.

Leah, the Biology Explorer, bounded in after him. She called her name and did her usual snappy salute. Leah knew all about plants and animals. Then came Ollie, dressed in the dark green shorts and T-shirt he wore to explore the rain forests.

"What's the mission?" Ollie asked.

"The Exploration Station hasn't told us yet," Roshni said.

"Kiki—here!" A girl zoomed through the doorway on a powered skateboard. Kiki was the Engineering Explorer, and Roshni knew she had built the skateboard herself.

Cheng, who was the Geology Explorer, came running in next. He was wearing a T-shirt that featured pictures of various colorful rocks. Gustavo, the History Explorer, followed him in, and the doorway winked shut.

All the Secret Explorers stood in a circle around the map on the floor. Any moment now, the Exploration Station would show them their mission.

Any moment now...

"Nothing's happening," Gustavo said. "The Exploration Station isn't broken, is it?"

"No way," Kiki said sternly.

"There's the answer, guys!" said Cheng with a laugh. He pointed up. "We're all looking in the wrong place."

They all gazed up at the Milky Way glowing on the ceiling. Roshni felt a rush of excitement. It was going to be a space mission—and she was the Space Explorer!

An image appeared among the stars in a little square window. It showed a shiny metal object with a large dish on the front. The object tracked slowly through the starry darkness.

"It's a probe!" Roshni said.

"A what?" asked Leah with a frown.

"A sort of spacecraft with no one on board. It's remote-controlled from a base back on Earth," Roshni explained. "Scientists send probes off into space to find things out. There must be a problem with this one!"

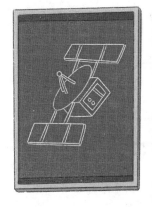

Now that they all knew what the mission was, there was only one more question— who would be picked to go? *I really hope it's me*, thought Roshni. They all stood still, waiting eagerly. Everyone knew that only two lucky Explorers would be chosen.

Roshni's compass badge lit up.

"Yes!" she cheered. "I'm going into space!"

Everyone laughed. "That's no surprise," Tamiko said with a smile. "You are the Space Explorer, after all!"

But it was Ollie whose badge lit up next.

He stared at it. "Uh... Roshni, are there any rain forests in space?"

"Not as far as we know," Roshni said.

"Don't worry," said Connor grinning. "The Exploration Station never gets it wrong. We all know that, right?"

"Right!" they all agreed. Even if they

didn't understand the Exploration Station's choices, it never let them down.

"Okay, guys. Ready to go?" Kiki rubbed her hands together. "I love this part!"

She went to the control panel and pushed a huge red button.

With a shudder of machinery, a platform rose up from below the floor. Sitting in the middle was a battered old go-kart with two plastic seats. It was named the Beagle, after the ship sailed by the great scientist Charles Darwin. The Secret Explorers knew that their Beagle was much more impressive than it looked.

All the Explorers who weren't going on the mission went and sat by their computers. The screens lit up, showing images of the solar system. Roshni knew that if she and Ollie needed any help during their mission, they could always call upon their friends.

BEEP-BOOP, said the Beagle. It seemed to be saying, "Hurry up!"

"Don't worry," Roshni said with a laugh. "We can't wait to get going, either."

She and Ollie climbed into their seats and buckled their safety harnesses. Roshni

took a deep breath and pressed the large, glowing button marked "START."

Instantly, there was a dazzling flash of light. With a deep humming, rattling sound, the Beagle began to transform while they were still sitting in it. The hard plastic seats swelled into padded ones. Banks of controls rose up before their astonished eyes.

The Beagle shot forward into a swirling tunnel of light that had appeared in front of them. It picked up speed, going faster and faster. The light became too bright to look at... and just like that, it faded away again.

Roshni looked around. Window panels, complicated controls, and a joystick had appeared in front of her. Everything was suddenly very quiet. A strange feeling came over her—a sort of floaty lightness.

Outside, stars glinted like diamonds against total blackness.

Her mouth opened with amazement. This was too good to be true.

"Is it nighttime already?" Ollie asked. "I can see stars outside."

"That's because we're in space," Roshni said triumphantly. "The Beagle has changed into a spaceship!"

Chapter Two
DANGER INCOMING

With a cheerful beep, a sign lit up that said, "UNFASTEN SEAT BELTS NOW". Roshni and Ollie glanced at each other and quickly undid their buckles.

"Might as well have a look around," Roshni suggested.

"Whoa!" Ollie cried. "What's going on? I'm flying!"

Sure enough, he was gently drifting up into the air. His unfastened seat belt rippled below him like a flag in the wind.

Roshni giggled. "You're not flying. You're floating!"

She pushed down with her hands, and immediately rose upward. Her hair wafted out around her as if she were underwater. It felt pretty strange, but very fun, too.

Ollie chuckled as he waved his arms and legs. "This is awesome!"

"It's because there's hardly any gravity up here," Roshni explained. "Back on Earth, the gravity is strong and pulls everything down.

That's why we don't float away."

"This is much more fun," said Ollie. "I'm going to do a cartwheel." He sent himself spinning across the cabin.

Roshni went one better, and launched into a triple forward somersault.

"Look out!" Ollie warned as Roshni tumbled past him.

CRASH!

She bumped into the side of the cabin and knocked a coil of electrical cable off the wall. But thanks to the special padding all around the inside of the Beagle, it didn't hurt at all. They could zoom around as much as they liked!

They floated around for a while, getting used to the strange weightless feeling. The Beagle helpfully lit up some grab handles that they could hold on to.

"So where are we?" Ollie wondered.

"Space!"

"Sure, but where in space? Mars? Venus? The moon?"

"Let's find out." Roshni reached for a grab handle and pulled herself toward the window.

She gasped. Looming up ahead was a gigantic planet with orange stripes and faint rings. "Jupiter!" she said.

When Roshni had seen the planet through her telescope, it had seemed no bigger than her thumbnail. Now it was so big she couldn't even see all of it.

Ollie whistled. "Now that's a big planet. I bet you could fit Earth inside there at least ten times."

"Try one thousand three hundred times," Roshni said in awe. "It's the biggest planet in the solar system." She grabbed Ollie's arm. "And look! There's the Great Red Spot!"

From this close, Roshni could make out the enormous storm easily. *This definitely makes up for not seeing it earlier*, she thought.

"Wow!" said Ollie. "It's all swirly, like a whirlpool."

There were smaller spots spinning across Jupiter, too. Roshni pointed them out to Ollie.

"They're all storms on Jupiter's surface, like we have on Earth," she explained. "The Great Red Spot's a storm as well. It's been going on for hundreds of years." She pointed to a tiny shining object. "Jupiter's got moons like we have, too."

Ollie's eyebrows shot up. "Moons? You mean, more than one?"

Roshni grinned and showed him more little objects. "That's a moon. And so's that, and that."

"Seriously?" Ollie asked. "How many moons does Jupiter have?"

"Oh, more than seventy," Roshni said casually.

Ollie stared at her. "Seventy?"

"Yep," said Roshni. "And the rings, of course."

"Wait, what?" Ollie peered through the window. "I thought it was just Saturn that had rings."

"Look more closely," said Roshni.

Sure enough, there were ghostly rings around Jupiter. They were faint and easy to miss at first.

"They look a bit like when light shines through dust," Ollie said.

"That's exactly what they're made from," said Roshni. "They're dust from Jupiter's moons."

The view of Jupiter wobbled as the Beagle rocked from side-to-side. The console let out a **BRUP-BOOP** sound. Roshni and Ollie looked at one another. It sounded like the Beagle was saying, "Uh-oh!"

"Something's wrong," Roshni said.

BREEE! replied the Beagle, and made a jangly noise like a mouse running up and down an electronic keyboard.

Using the handles on the walls, Roshni and Ollie clambered down to the navigation display. A blinking red dot was heading in their direction, fast.

Roshni tapped the screen to see what it was, and the display zoomed in. It showed a huge rock, easily three times the size of the Beagle.

"It's an asteroid!" she cried. "No wonder the Beagle is worried. We need to steer clear of that thing or it could smash right through the hull!"

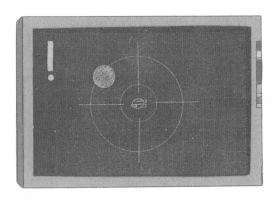

As quickly as they could, they climbed back into their seats and buckled themselves in tight.

Ollie turned to Roshni, looking anxious. "This might be a silly question, but... have you actually flown a spaceship before?"

"Only in my dreams," Roshni admitted.

She looked over the controls. She was sure she could figure out what to do, if she had enough time. But time was running out!

The Beagle blared a warning siren. Red lights flashed on the control console.

In the distance, the asteroid came into view, tumbling end over end. Roshni gulped.

"A little help here, Beagle?" she yelled.

Shiny arrow-shaped lights lit up, pointing to the controls they needed to use. Roshni took hold of the joystick, while Ollie grabbed the thruster levers that would power the spaceship forward. More lights sparked into life. There were switches to flick, buttons to press, and dials to turn.

All the time, the asteroid was coming closer and closer...

"We need to turn the nose to the left, then hit the thrusters," Roshni said.

"Got it," Ollie replied.

The Beagle beeped even louder than before. Now it was really worried. It sounded like an ambulance and a fire engine racing each other.

"Hang on, Beagle! We're doing our best!"

Roshni said through clenched teeth.

Using the joystick, she carefully nudged the spaceship's nose to the left. That should do it.

But to her horror, the ship kept on turning. If she didn't do something, it would just spin around on the spot!

She pushed the joystick the other way, just enough to stop the Beagle from spinning.

"Oh, no!" Ollie wailed. Roshni looked up.

The asteroid loomed up ahead of them, blotting out Jupiter. It was coming at them as fast as a speeding train.

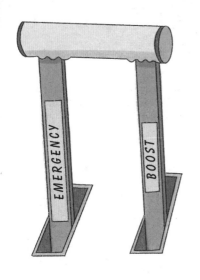

"Full thrust, now!" she yelled.

Ollie gritted his teeth and quickly hauled the big thruster controls down. Roshni yanked a lever labeled "EMERGENCY BOOST."

The Beagle shuddered as its powerful rocket engines roared into life. Roshni and Ollie were flung backward in their seats.

The asteroid went spinning past, so close it almost knocked off their tail fin.

They picked up speed. Soon the asteroid was far behind them—just a speck vanishing in the distance.

The Beagle made a happy *BEEP*. Roshni and Ollie cheered and slapped their hands together in a high five.

"That was way too close," Roshni said. "I don't mind studying space dust, but I don't want to become space dust!"

Chapter Three
TROUBLE IN SPACE

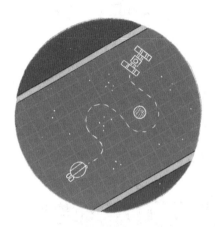

"Time to get on with the mission," said Roshni. A space probe needed the Secret Explorers' help. They didn't know what kind of help, but they knew it was urgent.

"Where's the probe?" Ollie asked.

Roshni peered out into space. "I can't see it. Hey, Beagle, can you scan for the probe?"

The Beagle was quiet for a few seconds.

Lights went on and off. Then it beeped a triumphant *TA-DAAAH!* An image of the probe appeared on the navigation display, as well as directions to reach it.

Roshni carefully pointed the Beagle's nose the right way and Ollie fired the rockets. Steadily, the spacecraft changed course.

"Flying a spaceship isn't as easy as it looks in the movies, is it?" Ollie said.

"That's because in space, if you set off in one direction, you continue moving that way and don't stop," Roshni explained. "You can't hit the brakes like you would in a car."

"So how do you slow down?"

"You have to turn on thrusters that fire in the opposite direction, so the movement cancels out," said Roshni.

"Got it," said Ollie. He turned to the navigation display. "Looks like we're heading the right way," he said. Next to the image of the probe, a distance counter was ticking down.

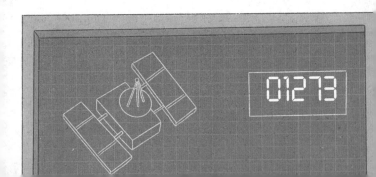

Something huge, gray, and round appeared in the distance. *Another asteroid?* wondered Roshni. *No—it's far too big!*

She quickly nudged the controls to steer them safely past it. As it rushed closer, she could make out craters on the surface.

"Hey, that looks like the moon!" Ollie said.

"It's a moon, all right," said Roshni. She'd figured out what they were looking at. "That's Ganymede, the biggest of Jupiter's moons."

"Is it bigger than our moon?"

Roshni laughed. "It's bigger than Mercury!"

"But Mercury's a planet!" Ollie said. "Wow! Seems like everything about Jupiter is king-size."

"That makes sense," Roshni said. "Jupiter gets its name from the king of the Roman gods, after all."

The Beagle made urgent little **BIP-BIP-BIP** noises. Roshni noticed that the distance counter was nearly at zero.

"We've almost reached the probe!" she said. "We need to slow down now. The Beagle should have retro-rockets somewhere—they fire in the direction a spaceship is flying, which slows it down."

"Got them!" Ollie pulled a lever. "Retro-rockets... fired!" he said. Steadily, the Beagle slowed to a complete stop.

The probe floated in space in front of them, gleaming in the light from the cockpit.

It looked very tiny against the gigantic planet in the background.

Roshni felt a sense of wonder at how far it had come. *It's probably been ten years since it blasted off from Earth*, she thought. *That's how long it takes to fly to Jupiter.* And now something had gone wrong. But what could it be?

She took a good long look at the probe. If only she'd brought some of her books on space exploration with her. The illustrations would have come in handy right now...

"There are the thrusters," she said, "and there's the power generator... and the camera. They all look fine. Oh, no! Ollie, look. The antenna is gone!"

"The what?" Ollie asked.

"The antenna. Space probes collect information, remember?" Roshni said. "But it's no good if the information just stays here on the probe. It has to be sent back to Earth."

"So the scientists can study it," said Ollie. "Hey, what do you think that's for?"

A clock had appeared on the control console. Bright red numbers flickered as it counted down the minutes and seconds.

"It looks like we've got just under two hours before something happens," Roshni said. She frowned. "But what?"

"It can't be a warning about the asteroid," Ollie said, "because we've already dodged it. Beagle, what's this countdown clock for?"

But all the Beagle did was beep noisily.

"The Beagle sounds pretty impatient," Roshni said. "Ollie, do you think the countdown has something to do with the probe?"

Ollie shrugged. "I don't know. And I don't think we're going to figure this one out on our own."

"You mean..."

Ollie nodded.

"Let's call the Exploration Station!" they said together.

Roshni operated the communications control. "Beagle calling the Secret Explorers! Do you copy? This is Roshni. We need help!"

There was silence for a second. Roshni bit her knuckles. Could the Beagle reach their friends back on Earth in time to fix the probe?

Then a crackly voice came through the speakers. "Leah here! Go ahead, Roshni. What's the problem?"

On the console, a screen flickered. Then an image of the Exploration Station appeared. Good work, Beagle! All the Secret Explorers were gathered around Leah's computer. They listened carefully as Roshni explained what was happening.

"Okay, everyone, go!" Connor said. "Research everywhere you can. Websites, records, the works. Roshni and Ollie are counting on us!"

Roshni and Ollie watched their friends eagerly. The Secret Explorers hurried to the other computer screens. Keyboards rattled as they typed, hunting for all the information they could find.

After only a few minutes, Roshni saw Cheng switch on his microphone. "Roshni, can you hear me?"

"Go ahead, Cheng," she replied.

"The probe's name is Odin," said Cheng. "Its mission is to watch a comet collide with Jupiter. The countdown clock is to tell you how long you have left before the comet hits. If you don't get it fixed in time..."

"... the probe's data will be lost," said Roshni. "And the scientists' work sending the probe into space will all be for nothing!"

Cheng nodded. "Good luck," he said.

"We know you can do it," added Kiki.

"Thanks for your help, guys," said Ollie. "Beagle out." He switched the radio off.

"We need to hurry," cried Roshni. "There are less than two hours left on the clock!" Frantically, she pressed switches and buttons. "There's no antenna, and the comet's coming, and we need to pix the frobe... I mean fix the probe..."

"Slow down," Ollie said. "Take deep breaths and imagine you're in a beautiful rain forest. It's what I do."

Roshni closed her eyes. She pictured tall, leafy trees—and felt much calmer. She opened her eyes again. "Thanks, Ollie!" She turned to the navigation screen. "Beagle," she said, "can you scan for the missing antenna like you scanned for the probe before?"

The Beagle beeped a cheery tune while its scanning dish whirred back and forth. **PING!** The antenna appeared on the screen.

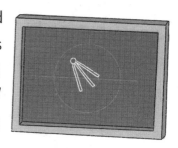

Roshni patted the console. "Nice job, Beagle." She peered through the window at a distant moon. It was white with red-brown streaks on its surface. "Looks like the antenna's in orbit around Europa."

"It's in Europe?" Ollie said. "You mean, back on Earth?"

"Not Europe! Europa, with an 'a' on the end." Roshni showed him. "It's nearly as big as Ganymede."

With the Beagle's help, Roshni and Ollie set a course for Europa.

As the little spacecraft zoomed toward it, Roshni glanced at the countdown clock. She shivered all over. Only an hour and a half left!

We've still got to grab that antenna and attach it to the Odin probe, thought Roshni. *Can we really do it in such a short time?*

Chapter Four
ONE GIANT LEAP...

Europa grew larger and larger as the Beagle drew closer. It looked like a frosty round ball against the endless blackness of space.

Roshni fired the retro-rockets to slow them down, and the Beagle began to orbit around the huge moon.

Ollie looked down at Europa's craggy surface. "I wouldn't go there for my vacation.

It looks like it's covered in ice."

"It is," Roshni said. "But it's only frozen on the surface. There are saltwater oceans under the ice."

Ollie raised his eyebrows. "Like we have on Earth?" he asked.

Roshni nodded. "Yes! And better still, scientists think there might even be some simple life-forms swimming around down there."

Ollie's mouth gaped open. "You mean… aliens?" he said.

"They would be tiny little microbes," Roshni explained. "You wouldn't be able to see them without a microscope. But, yes—we might be flying over alien life!" She got goose bumps just thinking about it.

"Cool!" Ollie spotted something and peered closer. "What's that thing? Did the aliens build it?"

Roshni saw it, too. It looked like a metal umbrella. She sat bolt upright. "That's the antenna from the Odin probe! Come on, we need to get it back!"

Working fast, the two of them flew the Beagle as close to the antenna as they could. They were getting more used to the controls now.

The antenna tumbled through space, high above the surface of Europa. Roshni wished she could just open a window and grab it, but that wasn't possible in a spaceship. All the air would rush out. This was going to be tricky.

"How are we going to get it?" Ollie wondered.

The Beagle made urgent beeps and wobbled around, jostling Roshni and Ollie in their seats.

"It's trying to tell us something!" Roshni said. "What is it, Beagle? Should we use a robot arm?"

FNAAARP! said the Beagle irritably.

"Can we pull it in with a tractor beam, or something?" Ollie guessed.

The Beagle flashed red lights in a big "X" on the dashboard and buzzed like computer-game sound effects.

No matter what Roshni and Ollie guessed, the Beagle just got more frustrated. It didn't want them to get the antenna with a harpoon gun, a big magnet, or a wad of chewing gum on the end of a string.

Roshni was rapidly running out of ideas— and the antenna was slowly dropping down toward Europa. If they didn't grab it in time, it would smash to pieces. She looked around the Beagle's cockpit to see if they'd missed anything.

Over to the right, she found a door she hadn't noticed before. She pressed a button and it slid open.

Inside was a compartment that was as tall as she was, containing two white space suits with round helmets.

"Wow!" she said.

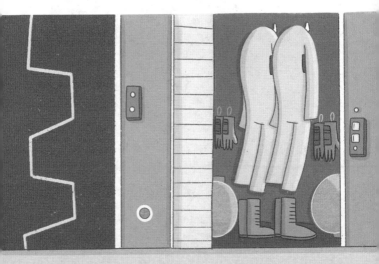

The Beagle made a very relieved beep. It sounded a lot like, "About time..."

Roshni and Ollie looked at one another. Roshni knew her friend was thinking the same thing—one of them had to stay inside the Beagle, but the other would have to put on a space suit and go outside, into space. It was dangerous, but it was also the chance of a lifetime.

"I'll go," they both said.

Ollie looked thoughtful for a moment. Then he said, "Actually, you should go, Roshni. You're the Space Explorer!"

Roshni grinned. "Thanks!"

She climbed out of her seat and slid her legs into the crumpled, shiny space suit. The Beagle lit up a panel that said "SAFETY INSTRUCTIONS." Ollie read them and made sure Roshni's suit was correctly prepared.

Roshni put her helmet on. Ollie checked that it was completely sealed. Even the tiniest gap or hole could result in Roshni's air supply being sucked out. She was breathless already, from sheer excitement. She could hardly believe this was real. She was about to do a space walk!

"This is your safety tether, okay?" said Ollie.

He held up a long cable. One end was securely fastened to the middle of Roshni's space suit, and the other ended in a clip. "Make sure the cable is always locked in place," Ollie said. "Then I can pull you back into the Beagle if anything goes wrong."

"Got it!" said Roshni.

The Beagle's airlock was behind the seats. Roshni knew an airlock was a chamber with an inner and an outer set of doors. You only ever opened one set at a time. This was to stop the air from leaving the spaceship.

She pulled the lever and the inner door opened with a hiss. She stepped into the cramped little chamber and closed the inner door behind her. Before she did anything else, she clipped her safety tether to the anchor point inside the airlock. Even if she got separated from the ship, the tether meant she'd always find her way back to the Beagle.

"Here we go," she whispered to herself. She remembered what Neil Armstrong had said when he became the first human being to walk on the moon: *One small step for a man, one giant leap for mankind...* A thrill passed through Roshni.

She pulled the second lever. Air rushed out of the airlock and the outer doors rumbled open.

There, in front of her, was the endless reach of starry space. She floated for a moment, just staring at it all in wonder.

Time to get on with the mission. The clock was ticking.

"One small step for a girl," Roshni murmured. "One giant leap for the Secret Explorers..."

She clambered unsteadily out of the airlock, using the outside of the Beagle like a jungle gym. It turned out to be trickier than she'd expected. The trouble with such little gravity was there was no such thing as "up"!

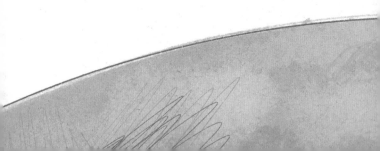

Roshni wasn't sure if it felt more like climbing up out of a hole, or sideways out of a door.

The antenna hung suspended in space only a few feet above the ship's nose. Roshni carefully worked her way toward it.

She had never seen such a spectacular view in all her life. Below her was the frozen, streaked surface of Europa, and away in the far distance was a shining dot. Roshni knew this was Saturn, the second biggest planet in the solar system.

The cockpit was below her now. She could see Ollie's anxious face looking out at her.

After carefully climbing across the outside of the Beagle, she finally got as close to the antenna as she could. She hung on to the Beagle with one hand and stretched up to grab the antenna with the other. But it was just out of reach.

She tried again, hoping to grab hold of the rim of its dish, but her gloved fingers closed on nothingness.

It was no good. Unless she let go of the Beagle, she'd never reach it.

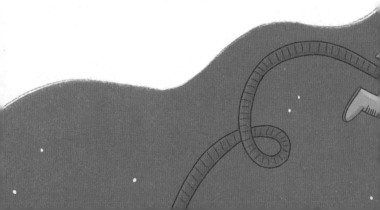

Roshni took a deep breath. She put her hands behind herself and pushed, as if she were launching off the edge of a swimming pool. She floated up in the direction of the antenna. The safety cable spooled out behind her.

Almost there. Just a little farther...

She stretched out toward the antenna with both hands—and grabbed it!

Chapter Five
SPACE SLINGSHOT

Roshni held the antenna tightly to her body. It was the same length as her arm. Up close, it looked even more like an umbrella.

Through the window of the Beagle, Roshni could see Ollie grinning and giving her a thumbs-up. She gave him one back.

"Just one problem now," she said to herself. "I've only got one hand free! So how am

I going to climb back inside the Beagle?"

A moment later, her question was answered. Her safety tether began to pull her back in. Ollie must have pressed the "RECALL" switch! She relaxed and let herself be reeled into the airlock, just like a fish on a line being pulled to shore.

In no time, she passed through the outer airlock doors. She shut them behind her and waited for the airlock to fill up with air again before unfastening her safety tether from the wall.

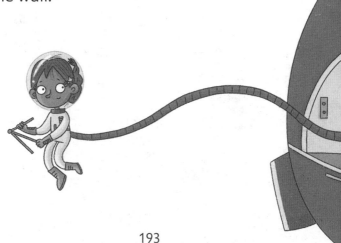

The inner doors slid open. There was Ollie, waiting with open arms. He gave her a hug. Roshni let go of the antenna so she could squeeze him back with sheer delight.

"You did a space walk!" he said. "That is so unbelievably cool!"

"I know," Roshni said happily. "I'll never forget it as long as I live."

In the background, the Beagle made happy burbling noises and blew a little trumpet fanfare.

"We'd better hurry back to the probe and repair it," Roshni said. "We've only got another thirty minutes before the comet's due to strike Jupiter."

She sat down at the controls and Ollie joined her. They set their course, fired the thrusters, and hoped they'd reach the Odin probe in time.

Through the window, they saw a cluster of shining shapes in the far distance. They were hurtling down toward the planet, leaving foggy trails behind them.

"There's the comet!" Roshni said.

"But it's all broken into bits," Ollie said, looking anxious. "Are we too late?"

"No," Roshni said excitedly. "Comets break up when they get close to a planet, because its gravity pulls them apart. This one must have broken up when it got close to Jupiter."

She checked the distance indicator. They were still nowhere near the probe. Only twenty minutes left to go!

"Can you go any faster, Beagle?" Roshni asked.

The Beagle made a sad beep.

Ollie patted the console. "It's okay. We know you're trying your best."

Roshni racked her brains. They needed to go faster. But how? She remembered watching an online video with her dad about space travel. She thought back to the part about something called "gravity assists"...

"That's it!" she yelled. "We can do a slingshot!"

"Sounds cool," said Ollie. "But what is it, exactly?"

"It's when we get caught in a planet or a moon's orbit on purpose, so we can speed up," Roshni said. "Scientists do it all the time with space probes, to save on fuel."

"I don't understand." Ollie frowned. "If we get caught in a planet's gravity, won't that slow us down?"

Roshni thought hard about how to explain it. "Okay. Say we're at a playground. I'm zipping around on my skates and you're going around in circles on a great big merry-go-round. Are you with me so far?"

"I guess," Ollie said.

"If I skate up behind you and you grab my hand for a second, and then let go, what happens?"

"I whiz you around for a little bit, then you zoom off really fast in a new direction!" Ollie burst out. "I get it. I'm the planet going around the sun, and me grabbing your hand is like gravity pulling you in."

"Exactly! Just like a planet giving a probe a speed boost."

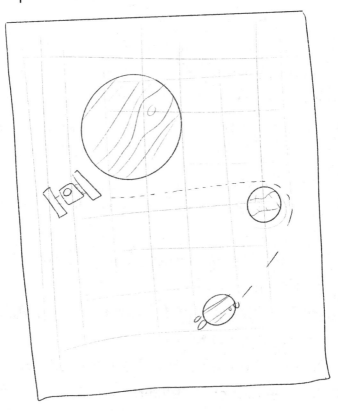

Ollie bent over the navigation screen. "So, all we have to do is find something that's already orbiting Jupiter and hitch a ride. Hey, how about this? It's got to be big enough."

Roshni looked over his shoulder. He was pointing at Io, another of Jupiter's largest moons. She hesitated. If they changed course now, they'd no longer be heading directly toward the probe. She knew she was taking a risk. But if she didn't, they might never get there on time.

She made her mind up. The risk was worth it.

"Beagle," she said, "can you steer us toward Io?"

The Beagle made a cheery beep that sounded a lot like "okeydokey!"

The steering jets fired, and the spacecraft lurched as it changed direction.

Roshni and Ollie watched Io appear in the distance. It grew larger with every passing second. Roshni gripped the joystick tightly. They needed to get caught in Io's gravity for long enough to speed up, then escape it again.

"We've got to time this just right," she said. "Too early, and we'll just shoot past. Too late, and the probe will get to watch us crashing..."

The Beagle bibbled nervously. Ollie stood by with his hand on the thruster control. The whole spacecraft vibrated as the engines thundered.

Roshni's mouth was dry. She steered the Beagle so it would come as close to Io as she dared. "Almost... almost... and here we go! Entering orbit now."

Io's gravity caught the little spacecraft in its grasp. Roshni and Ollie saw Io's surface zoom past them, blindingly fast.

On the dashboard, their velocity counter began to climb up and up, past the maximum limit and even higher.

"Punch it, Ollie!" she shouted.

Ollie hit the thrusters.

The Beagle broke free of Io's gravity and shot away.

They went screaming through space at mind-boggling speed. The velocity counter just read "ERROR." The Beagle squealed with delight.

Roshni held the joystick in a tight grip. Even though they were going so fast, time had almost run out. If they didn't reach the probe soon, all the work that had gone into it would be lost. And there would be no second chances...

Chapter Six
RACE AGAINST TIME

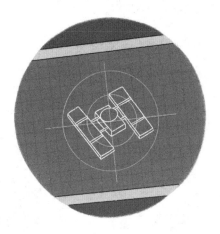

The Odin probe appeared on the scanner. Roshni watched anxiously as they hurtled toward it. They might make it in time... but it would be close!

The Beagle beeped a little tune as it rocketed along. "That slingshot move sped us up, but I think we might have overdone it," said Ollie. His eyes were wide. "We're going too fast!"

"Beagle, we need to slow down," Roshni warned.

The Beagle whined back at her. It clearly didn't want to slow down. It was too excited!

"I know you're having fun, but remember the mission!" she said.

With a sad-sounding beep, the Beagle turned on the retro-rockets. The velocity counter stopped flashing wildly and started to show actual numbers again. Gradually, their speed dropped until they were hovering at a standstill, right beside the gleaming Odin probe.

Ollie glanced at the mission timer. "Fifteen minutes left. Can you fix the probe in that time?"

"If I'm fast," Roshni replied. She was already pulling her helmet back on. "Wish me luck!"

Ollie grabbed her a tool kit from a compartment overhead. Roshni tucked it under her left arm, holding the antenna in her hand. She kept her right hand free to hold on to the Beagle.

She stood in the airlock and closed the inner doors. She was just reaching for the outer door switch when she remembered her safety tether!

That was a close one, she thought, as she clipped it in place.

"You okay in there?" came Ollie's voice through her helmet speaker.

"All ready," she said. "I didn't know we could talk to each other."

"Yeah, I think the intercom uses the safety tether as a communications cable," Ollie explained.

Knowing that she'd be able to stay in contact with Ollie made Roshni feel more confident.

She opened the outer doors. The probe was right there, hanging in space only a few yards away. Maybe this would be easier than she'd dared to hope.

Keeping a careful hold on the antenna and the tool kit, she pushed herself away from the Beagle.

The probe came within reach. Roshni grabbed one of the stronger-looking struts. Once she was sure she was secure, she moved the antenna into place.

She could see exactly what had happened. The antenna was held on by a sort of grip, and it was buckled and twisted where a meteor must have struck it. She'd have to replace it. Luckily, the tool kit had a spare.

"You always make sure we have what we need, don't you, Beagle?" she said fondly.

Ollie was watching her through the window, nervous as a cat in a lightning storm. "Ten minutes," he said.

Roshni focused her mind like never before. She took a wrench from the tool kit and undid the bolts holding the grip that had connected the antenna to the probe.

It was cracked—no wonder the antenna had floated off! Once she'd unscrewed it, the broken grip started to spin away. Roshni caught it and placed it in the tool kit. *Don't want to leave any litter behind*, she thought.

Next, she attached a new grip and bolted it on.

"Eight minutes," said Ollie. "You can do it!"

This next part was all-important. She slotted the antenna into the new grip, making sure the angle was exactly right. If it wasn't pointing the right way, the signals wouldn't reach Earth, and the data would be lost.

She quickly tightened the grip until it was secure.

"All done," she gasped.

She turned to the window, expecting to see Ollie's smiling face. But he wasn't smiling. His face was a mask of terror. His hands were white where they were pressed against the glass.

He yelled, "Roshni, get back to the ship! Now!"

She stared at him. This didn't make any sense.

Then she realized the Beagle was making a **SKREEE** sound of panic, too. *What could have scared them like this?*

She looked around—and in that instant, she had her answer.

As it plunged toward Jupiter, the shattered comet was shedding debris. A storm of tumbling, icy chunks were flying at her! They glittered, sharp as flint, in the light from the Beagle.

"I'm bringing you in," Ollie said firmly. He punched the "RECALL" button.

Roshni felt the reassuring tug of her safety tether pulling her back to the Beagle. She glanced fearfully at the oncoming shower of shards and told herself not to panic.

The first of the shards pinged off her helmet. More of them rattled and zinged around her.

Roshni tried to stay calm and breathe evenly. Soon she'd be back in the safety of the airlock...

"Are you okay?" Ollie said. "Roshni, talk to m—"

His voice cut out.

Roshni drifted toward the airlock door… and right past it.

"Ollie, pull me in!" she yelled. "What's going on? Can you hear me? Ollie!"

Why wasn't he answering?

She looked down. Pure horror ran through her. The safety tether had snapped clean off. One of the razor-sharp comet fragments had sliced right through it.

Now she was slowly drifting farther and farther away from the Beagle. That was how things worked in space, she knew. Once you started moving in one direction, you kept going that way forever and ever...

Roshni gulped. *How am I going to get back to the Beagle now?*

Chapter Seven
LOST IN THE STARS

Roshni was spinning head over heels, as if she were on a crazy fairground ride that she couldn't escape. The stars wheeled around her.

"Don't panic," she said aloud to herself. "Whatever you do, don't panic."

But it was very hard not to, with her stomach doing somersaults and the Beagle drifting steadily away.

Every time she flipped over, she saw the same things pass by. She glimpsed the Beagle, the Odin probe, Jupiter, and the comet fragments about to crash into it. It was making her feel dizzy. If only there were some way she could stop spinning, or something she could grab hold of!

What was it Ollie had said? Imagine you're in a beautiful rain forest. Take deep breaths... Well, it had worked before, hadn't it?

She took a deep breath—and suddenly she realized she was in even more danger than she'd known.

The only air she had to breathe was the air in her suit tanks. She didn't even know how much of it was left after her first space walk. An hour? Or only a few minutes?

"I'm not going to panic," she whispered. "I'm a Secret Explorer. I'll find a way out of this, somehow..."

It didn't seem like things could possibly get any worse. But they did.

She saw the airlock doors on the Beagle close.

Roshni felt cold all over. *Now I'll never get back inside...*

But just as she was on the verge of giving up hope, they opened again. There was Ollie standing in the airlock, wearing the second space suit!

With one hand, he was waving to Roshni. In his other hand, he was holding something like a long rope. *Where did he find that?* Roshni wondered. She hadn't seen a rope on board the Beagle.

Ollie spun the rope's end around and let go of it. It came uncoiling toward Roshni, wobbling and wavering through space. She lost sight of it as she spun all the way over yet again.

As she came back around, she saw the rope was getting closer.

On her next flip, it was closer still.

After one more spin, it would be close enough to catch!

She reached out, her hand open as she turned another full circle. There was the rope, drifting right by her head.

She grabbed the rope, wrapped it around her waist and tied it securely.

"Phew!" she sighed.

Ollie backed into the airlock, where red warning lights were furiously blinking. Roshni watched as he took hold of the rope with both hands and began to pull.

Slowly but surely, Ollie hauled Roshni back toward the airlock.

The moment she was all the way inside, Ollie punched the door control and the outer doors slid shut. The airlock's red warning lights turned green.

Roshni gave him a huge, slightly awkward hug. It wasn't easy to hug someone when you were wearing a big, bulky space suit! Ollie hugged her back as best he could.

The inner doors opened to let them back into the cockpit. The Beagle filled the screens with smiley-face emojis and made happy, excited beeps that sounded like puppies playing.

Roshni pulled her helmet off and shook her hair free. She took a big gasp of air.

"Thanks, Ollie," she said. "I owe you one!"

"Any time," Ollie beamed, taking off his helmet.

Roshni looked down at her waist, where Ollie's rope was still tied. Now she could get a good look at it, she could see it was made of electrical wires wound together. So he hadn't found a spare rope—he'd made one!

"Where did you get the idea to do this?" she asked him.

"In the rain forest. Where else?" He laughed. "We weave vines together to make ropes when we're out exploring. One wire by itself wouldn't have been strong enough to pull you in, but lots of them woven together worked just fine."

Roshni grinned. "See? The Exploration Station always picks the right Explorers for every mission!"

Ollie grinned back.

Together, they looked out of the window at the Odin probe, which had turned to record the comet crash into Jupiter. The comet fragments were zooming toward the gigantic planet.

"We're just in time to see the collision!" said Ollie.

Chapter Eight
JUPITER'S FIREWORKS

Roshni and Ollie had front-row seats for the most spectacular cosmic fireworks display they could ever hope to see. They looked out through the spacecraft's windshield, breathless with excitement. The last few seconds were ticking away on the countdown clock.

"Three, two, one... zero!" Roshni yelled.

The first of the comet fragments plunged into Jupiter's atmosphere. A tremendous fireball erupted at the point of impact. Roshni shielded her eyes. This was amazing!

Enormous shock waves went rippling out across Jupiter's surface, like rings spreading out on a lake.

"How come we can't hear it?" Ollie asked. "An explosion that size ought to be deafening us!"

"Because sound waves need air to travel, and there isn't any air in space," Roshni explained.

The next fragment went tumbling down into the seething storm. Another gigantic explosion went up.

"Look at that," Ollie said. "I bet the ground's shaking down there!"

"Jupiter's not solid—it's made of gas," Roshni said. "It might be solid right at the core, but scientists aren't sure about that. There's a lot scientists don't know about space, which is why they need probes like Odin to do investigations."

Another fireball expanded across Jupiter's surface. Ollie whistled. "Just imagine if a comet hit Earth!"

"A comet did hit Earth, millions of years ago," Roshni explained. "Well, scientists think it was either a comet or a meteorite. That's why the dinosaurs were all wiped out. The impact shook up our entire planet."

"Whoa, really?"

"The crater's still there, in Mexico," Roshni said. "Ask Tamiko about it!"

Outside, the Odin probe was busily collecting data. Its camera was recording image after image, capturing the moment the comet smashed into Jupiter.

That gave Roshni an idea. "Hey, Beagle, can you tune in to the probe's broadcast channel? We might be able to listen in."

BEEEEEEP-BOOP! chirped the Beagle. It sounded like, "Sure thing!"

The computer screens in front of them filled up with information. Roshni grinned. They were getting to watch a science broadcast as it happened and learn cool stats just like the scientists back on Earth!

"Look how fast that comet was going when it hit!" Ollie said. "134,000 miles per hour!"

Roshni's mind boggled. An Olympic athlete running a hundred-meter dash would get up to about 28 miles per hour. The speedometer in her parents' car only went up to about 110 miles per hour. The speed of sound itself was a stunning 767 miles per hour. But the comet was going more than one hundred and seventy times faster than sound!

"No wonder the fragments exploded like that!" she said. "Hey, how hot were those fireballs, anyway?"

Ollie tapped the screen and looked confused. "I'm not sure the probe's working right. These figures are incredible."

"Incredible how?"

"Apparently the temperature down there reached 42,700°F!"

"Forty-two thousand degrees?" Roshni struggled to imagine how hot that was. She knew water boiled at 212°F, but that seemed puny by comparison. So, she said "Beagle, can you show us some temperatures to compare that with?"

The Beagle flashed up some figures for them to read. Iron boiled at 5,184°F—so the comet's impact was about nine times hotter than boiling iron.

"Wow!" Roshni said.

"What about the Earth's core?" Ollie suggested. "That's liquid rock, so it's got to be seriously hot."

They were amazed to see that the center of the Earth measured 10,800°F. The comet explosion was more than four times hotter than the core of their own planet!

"I'm glad we're up here in the Beagle, safely out of the way," Ollie said. "If we were any closer we might be burned to ashes!"

They watched in wonder as the last of the fragments burned up in Jupiter's atmosphere. Roshni saw the information flicker across the screen and smiled. The scientists back on Earth would learn a lot from the probe's data. Maybe what they learned would help humans travel to other planets in the future. Maybe she'd be on one of those spaceships as a grown-up astronaut...

The Beagle beeped. The big button that had read "START" now read "HOME."

"Mission complete," said Roshni. "Time to go back!"

They buckled their safety harnesses and Roshni pressed the button.

Just as it had before, the Beagle shot forward into a tunnel of white light. It was so bright, Roshni could hardly look at it. She thought she could see stars whizzing past, leaving rainbow-colored trails.

Only moments later, the light faded and they slowed to a stop.

The controls and instrument panels were gone. The Beagle was just a go-kart again, with old plastic seats and wacky handlebars. It looked more like something you would find in a backyard shed than a spacecraft that had just been in orbit around Jupiter.

Roshni unfastened her harness and stretched. She looked around the familiar Exploration Station. It was good to be back safe and sound. *But I miss being in space already!* she thought.

All the other Secret Explorers came crowding around. They gave Roshni and Ollie hugs and high fives. Everyone had dozens of questions about the mission.

"Were you scared?" asked Gustavo.

"What was the comet like?" Cheng wanted to know.

"Did you see any aliens?" asked Leah.

Roshni thought of the tiny microbes that might be under the frozen seas of Europa. "Maybe," she said.

"So did you bring anything back for the display cabinets?" Tamiko asked.

Roshni groaned. "Oh, no! I didn't think of that!"

But Ollie leaned over and pulled something from between the Beagle's handlebars. "Hey, Roshni?" he said. "Is this what I think it is?"

He held up a lump of gray ice. It was beginning to melt under the bright lights of the Exploration Station. Inside the ice was a dark shape.

Roshni gasped. "It's a shard of the comet! It must have gotten jammed in the Beagle. I guess we did bring something back after all!"

The ice melted away, revealing a chunk of what looked like dark, bumpy rock. "Wow!" everyone said as they looked at it closely.

"Comets are mostly made of ice," Roshni explained. "But there are minerals and other things inside them, too."

She opened the display cabinet and placed the comet shard inside. It sat between one of Tamiko's fossils and an insect embedded in amber that Ollie had found in the rain forest.

It was time for Roshni to go back to her camping trip. Her parents probably thought she was taking a nap in her tent. *What would they say if they knew I'd been on a space walk?* she thought.

"Goodbye, everyone!" Roshni called. "See you next time!" She waved to her Secret Explorer friends and stepped through the glowing door. She came out the other side and found herself outside her tent. She was back in the Himalayas, by the shores of the lake, encircled by the mountains. Beside the campfire, her parents were still talking—no time had passed while Roshni had been away on her mission.

"Almost forgot what I came to the tent for," she said to herself, and laughed. She ducked inside, then rummaged through her things and found the extra-powerful lens for her telescope.

Her telescope was right where she'd left it—sitting on its tripod and pointing at the sky. She screwed the new lens in and took a fresh look at Jupiter. Much better! The planet stood out bright and clear. The telescope had made it large enough for her to see the Great Red Spot now.

Roshni could hardly believe she'd seen Jupiter up close, and even looked down into its enormous, raging, swirling storm. She wondered what amazing sights her next Secret Explorers adventure would bring.

It was bound to be a big surprise. It always was.

And she couldn't wait for it to begin!

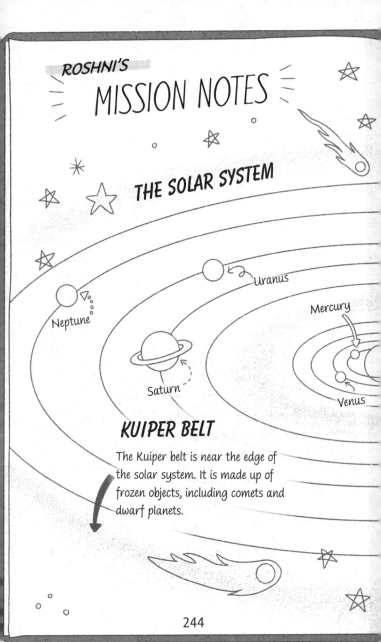

MISSION NOTES

THE SOLAR SYSTEM

Neptune

Uranus

Saturn

Mercury

Venus

KUIPER BELT

The Kuiper belt is near the edge of the solar system. It is made up of frozen objects, including comets and dwarf planets.

The solar system began 4.6 billion years ago. A cloud of gas and dust was pulled together by gravity, eventually becoming a star—our sun. The bits of material left over clumped together into bigger and bigger pieces, forming planets, asteroids, comets, and moons. They all orbit, or travel around, the sun.

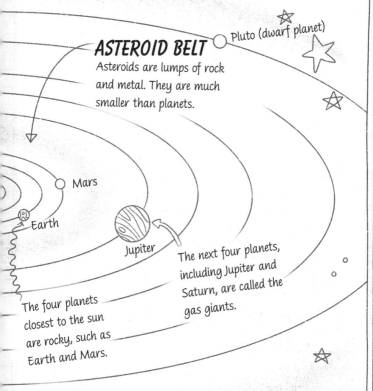

Pluto (dwarf planet)

ASTEROID BELT
Asteroids are lumps of rock and metal. They are much smaller than planets.

Mars

Earth

Jupiter

The next four planets, including Jupiter and Saturn, are called the gas giants.

The four planets closest to the sun are rocky, such as Earth and Mars.

Use this handy phrase to remember the order of the planets from the sun:
My **V**ery **E**ducated **M**other **J**ust **S**erved **U**s **N**achos.

JUPITER

Jupiter is the largest planet in our solar system. It is mostly made of the gas hydrogen and does not have a solid surface.

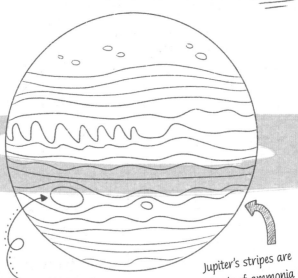

GIANT RED SPOT

Jupiter's Great Red Spot is a gigantic spinning storm. It's twice the size of Earth and has raged for hundreds of years.

Jupiter's stripes are clouds of ammonia and water. The clouds are very cold and windy.

246

FACT FILE

Earth

Jupiter

* **Size**: Jupiter is the largest planet in the solar system. You could fit 1,321 Earths inside Jupiter! If Earth were the size of a grape, Jupiter would be the size of a basketball.

* **Distance from Sun**: Jupiter orbits about 484 million miles (778 million km) from the sun. Earth is 94 million miles (150 million km) away from the sun.

Jupiter's rings are made of dust.

* **Moons**: Scientists now think Jupiter has 79 moons, but they're finding more all the time. The four biggest moons are Ganymede, Io, Callisto, and Europa.

* **Length of a day**: A day on Jupiter only lasts 10 hours—this is how long it takes to rotate on its axis.

A YEAR ON JUPITER IS THE SAME LENGTH AS 12 EARTH YEARS!

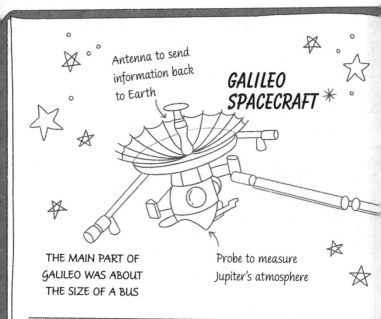

Antenna to send information back to Earth

GALILEO SPACECRAFT

THE MAIN PART OF GALILEO WAS ABOUT THE SIZE OF A BUS

Probe to measure Jupiter's atmosphere

MISSION TIMELINE

October 18, 1989
Galileo launches from Kennedy Space Center

February 10, 1990
Slingshots past Venus, using the planet's gravity to boost its speed

December 8, 1990
Flies by Earth, using its gravity to build speed

August 28, 1993
Visits an asteroid called Ida, discovering that it has its own tiny moon

July 22, 1994
Observes comet fragments impact Jupiter

THE GALILEO MISSION

Four spacecraft had previously flown by Jupiter, but Galileo was the first to orbit the planet. Galileo studied Jupiter and its moons and sent information back to Earth. When a comet collided with Jupiter, Galileo recorded valuable information about the event.

Antenna to gather information

September 7, 1996
Discovers that Europa, one of Jupiter's biggest moons, has an ocean of water

September 21, 2003
Plunges into the blazing hot atmosphere of Jupiter and is destroyed

December 7, 1995
Enters orbit around Jupiter. A probe descends into the atmosphere and sends back data for an hour before it is destroyed.

October 15, 2001
Makes closest flyby of Io, passing just 112 miles (180km) above the surface

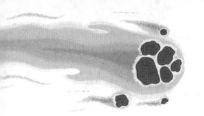

QUIZ

1   What's the name of the giant storm on Jupiter?

2   How many times could Earth fit into Jupiter?

3   Does Jupiter have rings?

4   How many moons does Jupiter have?

5   What is Jupiter's largest moon called?

6   Which of Jupiter's moons has got saltwater oceans?

7   Who was the first human being to walk on the moon?

8   What is the temperature at the center of the Earth?

SEARCH FOR JUPITER!

There are nine hidden Jupiter stickers to spot in this book. Can you find them all?

The stickers look like this!

Check your answers on page 255

GLOSSARY

AIRLOCK
a special chamber that stops air from escaping from inside a spaceship into space

ANTENNA
a device used to transmit and receive radio signals

ASTEROIDS
small rocky objects that orbit the sun

COCKPIT
area near the front of a spacecraft where the pilot controls the craft

COMETS
lumps of ice and dust in space

GRAVITY
a force that pulls objects together. The Earth's gravity keeps us on the ground!

METEORITE
a piece of
space debris
that has smashed
into a planet's
surface

MICROBES
tiny living
creatures that
can only be
seen with a
microscope

MICROSCOPE
a scientific
instrument used
to see tiny objects

MILKY WAY
the galaxy that
contains our
solar system

ORBIT
the path of an
object around a
star, planet, or moon

PROBE
an unmanned
robotic spacecraft
that explores space

TELESCOPE
a tool that allows
people to see
faraway objects

THE GREAT RED SPOT

a giant storm in Jupiter's atmosphere

RETRO-ROCKETS

rockets attached to a spacecraft that help slow it down

SHOCK WAVES

a special, very strong, type of vibration coming from one spot

SLINGSHOT

when a spacecraft uses the gravity of a planet to increase its speed

SOLAR SYSTEM

the system of planets and other objects orbiting the sun

SPACE DUST

dust in space from comets, asteroids, and stars. Jupiter's rings are made of dust

SPACE SUIT
a suit worn by
astronauts that
allows them to
survive in space

SPACE WALK
when astronauts
go outside their
spacecraft

VELOCITY
the speed of
an object in
one direction

Quiz answers
1. The Great
   Red Spot
2. 1,321
3. Yes
4. 79
5. Ganymede
6. Europa
7. Neil Armstrong
8. 10,800°F

THE SECRET EXPLORERS AND THE TOMB ROBBERS

Chapter One
BACK IN TIME

I love it when the museum is busy! thought Gustavo. All around him, people were admiring statues and peering into glass cases full of amazing objects from the past. He straightened his "Volunteer" armband.

"Excuse me!" called a cheerful woman in a blue jacket. She pointed to a globe-shaped vase. It was black and decorated with cream swirls. "Do you know how old this is?" she asked.

"It's probably about a thousand years old," Gustavo replied. "It was made by the Marajoara people. They lived on an island at the end of the Amazon River, right here in Brazil."

"That's really interesting," said the woman. "Thanks for your help!"

"No problem," said Gustavo with a grin.

The museum was close to his Rio de Janeiro home, so he'd been coming as long as he could remember. He knew so much about the objects on display that he could answer any question the visitors asked! He loved history and enjoyed helping to care for the artifacts other civilizations had left behind. *It would be amazing to go back in time*, Gustavo thought, *and see these objects being used by real ancient people!*

Out of the corner of his eye, he noticed a light shimmering. Gustavo's heart leaped. *Could it be...?* He turned around. On the elevator door was a glowing circle with the letters N, E, S and W. It was a compass!

Gustavo knew what it meant—a new mission for the Secret Explorers!

He hurried to the elevator, tingling with

excitement. The doors slid open by themselves and Gustavo stepped inside. All around him was a brilliant white light.

Wind whipped around Gustavo. It made him feel as if he were whizzing through the brightness. Then a moment later the light faded. Gustavo was back at the Exploration Station!

It had gleaming black stone walls, a map of the world on the floor, and a huge picture of the Milky Way on the ceiling. There was a line of computers along one wall.

"Gustavo— here!" he called.

A girl wearing a leaf-green T-shirt and a boy with red hair jumped up from a squishy sofa. They both grinned.

"Hi Leah," said Gustavo. "Hi Ollie!"

"I was just showing Ollie my new book about beetles," said Leah. She was the Biology Explorer, and knew all about plants and animals. Ollie was wearing a shirt with a parrot pattern—he was the team's rainforest expert.

Soon the other Secret Explorers arrived through the white glowing doorway, one after the other.

A girl skateboarded in. "Kiki—here!" She was the Engineering Explorer, and had made the skateboard herself.

"Cheng—here!" He was passionate about rocks and volcanoes.

Next came a girl with short dark hair who knew everything about dinosaurs. "Tamiko—here!"

"Roshni—here!" said the Space Explorer. She glanced up at the Milky Way on the ceiling.

"Connor—here!" said the ocean expert.

They all gathered excitedly around the map on the floor. Gustavo felt a swirl of

excitement in his middle. The Exploration Station would soon tell them about the mission!

"Where will it be?" Cheng wondered. His eyes sparkled as he watched the map.

"There!" Connor pointed. "Near the Mediterranean Sea!"

A pinpoint of light had appeared on the map. It grew and shimmered.

"The mission's in Egypt!" said Gustavo. "Right beside the River Nile!"

A screen projected up from the map. It showed the inside of a museum, and a man and woman in fancy uniforms. *They must be the curators who work there*, Gustavo thought. He listened eagerly to what they were saying.

"We just don't get enough visitors," the woman said sadly. She dusted a glass case containing a scarab beetle made of blue stone. *"This amulet from Pharaoh Khufu's pyramid is our only real treasure. But it's not enough to bring people in."*

The man sighed. *"You're right,"* he said. *"If only Khufu's treasures hadn't been looted by tomb robbers, we'd have a much better display."*

"We don't have any choice," the woman said. *"We'll have to close down the museum..."*

The screen disappeared.

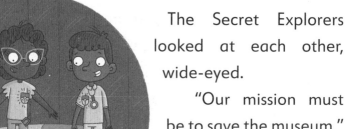

The Secret Explorers looked at each other, wide-eyed.

"Our mission must be to save the museum," said Ollie.

Roshni pointed to Gustavo. "It's your mission! Your badge is glowing."

Gustavo felt a rush of excitement. He adored museums. *We can't let the one in Egypt close down*! he thought.

"That makes sense," said Tamiko. "You're the History Explorer, after all."

"Hey, my badge is glowing," said Kiki. "I wonder how engineering can help the museum?"

"We know the Exploration Station always chooses the right team," said Leah.

"True!" agreed Kiki. She went over to the computers and pressed a button. A hatch in the floor opened and up rose the Beagle. It looked like an old go-kart, with two battered seats and a wobbly steering wheel. *But it won't stay like that*, Gustavo thought.

The Beagle was named after the ship that carried a famous scientist, Charles Darwin, on a voyage of discovery. What were he and Kiki going to discover? Gustavo couldn't wait to find out!

Everyone took their places at the computer screens while he and Kiki climbed onto the Beagle. Gustavo pressed the "GO" button. The Beagle shook and rattled as if it was falling apart. The wheels disappeared and wooden panels rose around them. In a flash of light, the Beagle jerked forward. Gustavo clutched the sides. They whooshed

through dazzling whiteness, then after a few moments the light faded. The Beagle was bobbing gently up and down—on water!

"It's transformed into a boat! We're on a river!" said Gustavo.

Kiki's eyes shone. "It must be the Nile!"

Gustavo shaded his eyes from the hot sun and looked to shore. Two gigantic, triangular

white shapes gleamed in the heat. "You're right!" he gasped. "Those are pyramids!"

"Wow!" said Kiki. "They're bigger than I ever imagined! It's almost like they're touching the sky."

Gustavo's eyes grew wide. "Hold on! There are supposed to be three pyramids... and one of these is only half finished..." His tummy did a flip. "Kiki... we've gone back in time—to ancient Egypt!"

Chapter Two
RESCUE ON THE NILE

"This is fantastic!" said Gustavo, leaping up. "I've always wanted to see an ancient civilization—and now I'm in ancient Egypt, on the River Nile!"

Kiki clutched the side of the Beagle, which was wobbling around. "We'll be *in* the Nile if you don't sit down," she said. "But Gustavo, are you sure this is *really* ancient Egypt?"

Gustavo watched, spellbound, as two fishermen pulled a net full of splashing fish ashore. Nearby, a girl was washing her hair at the water's edge. People in tunics and sandals sat in the doorways of white flat-roofed houses, or in the shade of rustling palm trees.

He grinned at Kiki. "I'm sure. We're in the time of the pharaohs—the rulers of ancient Egypt!"

"Awesome!" Kiki said. "But how will being in ancient Egypt help us save the museum? It doesn't even exist yet."

Gustavo sat down on a wooden bench.

"The Exploration Station must have sent us here for a reason. Let's go and find out what it is."

A flapping noise made him look up. A square-shaped sail billowed open above them.

"The Beagle wants to set off too," Gustavo said. "But I have no idea how to sail a boat!"

"I'll figure it out!" Kiki twanged a rope attached to the sail. "Okay, the sail moves like that..." She shifted to where a large oar was fastened to the back of the boat. "And this is a sort of rudder, for steering..."

Gustavo explored the Beagle, too. Tucked under the bench was what looked like a toolbox. Gustavo opened it up, and the Beagle gave a burst of excited electronic beeps.

They sounded very out of place on the ancient Nile.

"Quiet," Gustavo said with a laugh. "We don't want anyone to realize we're from the future!" He saw that the lid of the box was a screen, with a microphone and a row of buttons. "It's a communications panel," he told Kiki.

"Great!" Kiki said. "That means we can call the Exploration Station if we need help."

"Even though they're thousands of years ahead of us," added Gustavo. "You're amazing, Beagle!"

The Beagle gave a smug beep.

Gustavo found a waterproof bag tucked by the communications panel. It contained tunics, belts, and sandals. "We'd better put these on before we meet any ancient

Egyptians," he said. "They might think our jeans and sneakers are little strange."

After they had changed, Kiki held tightly to the ropes that controlled the sail while Gustavo took hold of the rudder. The wind filled the sail and the Beagle glided along the Nile.

They both looked up in awe as they drew closer to the pyramids. They were so huge, the people dotted around them looked as tiny as ants. There were smaller buildings and walls around them, too. "I never knew the pyramids were white," said Kiki. "I always thought they were the color of sand."

"They're covered with polished limestone," said Gustavo. "By our time, the limestone will have gone, and pollution will have made the stone blocks underneath darker."

Kiki pointed to a giant statue. It looked like a resting lion, but with a human head. "Hey, isn't that the Great Sphinx? I've seen pictures of it, but it didn't have a nose."

"It broke off," Gustavo said. He was so excited to see the Sphinx with a complete face! "No one knows what happened to it. And there's an Anubis!"

He pointed to a statue standing among the various buildings. The statue had a human body and a head similar to a dog's.

"Was Anubis one of the pharaohs?" asked Kiki.

Gustavo shook his head. "He was one of the gods worshipped by the ancient Egyptians," he said. "They believed he was in charge of death and the afterlife."

"He's got a jackal's head," said Kiki. "I've seen those at home in Ghana... Hold on, the wind's changed direction!"

Kiki pulled on a rope to swing the sail around. Gustavo adjusted the rudder and the Beagle picked up speed. Ahead was a wooden dock jutting out into the river. A large ship was moored there. Gustavo saw that the ship's decks were stacked with blocks of stone.

"Those are for building the pyramid," he said.

Dozens of men were unloading the stones. Several more walked up and down, shouting orders. The men used long poles to move the blocks onto ramps.

"They're using the poles as levers," said Kiki. "Levers increase the amount of force you're able to create, which is why they can lift those huge lumps of stone." She grinned. "It's ancient engineering!"

A small boat was coming toward them, rowed by a boy about their own age. He was surrounded by packages and bags stuffed with scrolls. He suddenly stopped rowing

and started scooping water out of his boat with a wooden bucket.

"Great goddess Bastet!" the boy exclaimed, looking up at the sky. "Can't you stop the water coming in?"

"Hey!" Kiki yelled. "Do you need help?"

"Yes!" the boy shouted. "All my stuff's going to get soaked!"

Gustavo steered the Beagle until they were alongside the boy's boat. He leaned over the side and used his hands to help scoop out the water.

"Thanks for helping," the boy gasped.

"I'm worried that the honey Mom wanted will end up at the bottom of the Nile!"

"What's your boat made of?" Kiki asked.

The boy stared. "Papyrus, of course."

Kiki looked confused.

"It's a kind of paper," Gustavo whispered. "Ancient Egyptians made it from reeds."

"Perfect," Kiki said. She rummaged under the bench on the Beagle and pulled out a wooden bowl. "Your mom's honey," she said to the boy. "Can I use some? And one of those scrolls? I need them to patch up your boat!"

"How can honey mend the hole?" wondered the boy, but he passed over a small jar made from pottery and a papyrus scroll.

Working quickly, Kiki poured some honey into the

bowl. She unrolled the scroll and used her fingers to smear the paste all over it. Then she climbed into the boy's boat and pressed it firmly over the hole.

"It's not perfect," she said, "but it should hold until you reach the dock."

The boy grinned with relief. "Amazing! Thank you so much!"

Kiki climbed back into the Beagle and they followed the boy into the dock, just in case Kiki's papyrus patch sprang a leak. Once both boats were tied up, Gustavo and Kiki helped the boy unload his scrolls and packages.

"I'm really glad you were on the Nile today," the boy

said. "My name's Bek." His head was shaved except for one lock of hair on the side. He had a battered leather bag slung across his body.

"I'm Kiki," Kiki told him, "and this is Gustavo."

"Those aren't Egyptian names," said Bek. "Where are you from?"

"A long way away," said Gustavo. "We're from... er... Discoveria."

The boy tilted his head, looking puzzled. Before he could ask any more questions, Kiki said, "Shall we help you carry your stuff home?"

"That would be great!" said Bek delightedly. Once he'd handed them some bags filled with scrolls, he heaped everything else into his bag, picked up a big sack of flour, and set off.

Gustavo and Kiki followed. They passed people moving more stone blocks, merchants carrying bread and linen, and children playing with wooden toy crocodiles.

"Let's keep an eye out for clues about our mission," Gustavo whispered to Kiki.

Kiki nodded. "Maybe helping Bek will somehow help the museum."

They passed the statue of Anubis with its strange jackal head. A shadow flickered beside it, and Gustavo had the feeling he was being watched. He spun around to

look—and saw a tall woman in a long white shawl that swooped behind her. But the next moment, she had gone.

Bek glanced at him. "Are you okay?" he asked.

"I thought someone was following us," Gustavo said. "But I must have imagined it..."

Chapter Three
STOLEN!

Bek's home was larger than the ones along the riverbank. Its flat roof had a canopy, making a shady area to sit. Gustavo knew that the family would sleep up there on hot nights.

"It seems to be built of bricks," Kiki whispered, sounding surprised. "And the windows are tiny!"

"They're not like our bricks," Gustavo whispered back. "They're made of mud and straw. And the windows are small and high up, to keep out the heat and dust."

Bek led them up to the house. Three men hurried past, carrying armfuls of white linen. "They work for my grandfather," Bek explained. "He's a mummifier."

Gustavo felt a thrill of excitement. He knew the ancient Egyptians mummified the dead to preserve their bodies, because they believed they would need them in the afterlife.

"My grandfather was in charge of mummifying Pharaoh Khufu's body," said Bek. "See the biggest pyramid? Khufu's mummy is buried in there."

Kiki nudged Gustavo. "The people from the museum spoke about Khufu," she whispered. "Maybe we're about to find out how to complete our mission!"

They followed Bek up a ramp, through the front door, and into a large room. There were shelves piled with scrolls. Blocks of ink stood on a table beside a stack of brushes.

"These are our writing materials," Bek explained, as they all put down their bags.

Kiki picked up some round objects. "What are these?" She sniffed them. "Mmm, they smell like cinnamon."

"They're incense pellets," said Bek. "I like to burn them while I practice writing. The scent helps me concentrate. Here, take a couple."

"Thanks!" Kiki tucked two incense pellets into her belt. "I'll use these when I'm building things."

Just then Gustavo's eye was caught by a sheet of papyrus on another table. On it were drawings of a frog and a bird. "Those are hieroglyphs, aren't they, Bek?" he said. "Egyptian writing?"

Bek was stacking scrolls in a basket woven from rushes. He glanced around.

"That's right. They look like pictures, but most of them stand for a sound. Don't you have hieroglyphs in Discoveria?"

"Where?" said Kiki.

Gustavo nudged her.

"Oh, right, Discoveria," she said. "No, we write with joined-up letters."

"So do I, in school," said Bek. "That's called hieratic writing, and it's quicker than

writing in hieroglyphs." He sighed. "But I really want to train to be a scribe, and write perfect hieroglyphs." He pulled a sheet of papyrus from a box under the table. "I'm learning, though. Look."

The papyrus was completely covered with Bek's attempts at hieroglyphs. Most were smudged, but Gustavo could make out birds, snakes, feathers, and a lot of legs.

"I want to write as well as this," Bek said, taking a scroll from the back of a shelf. He unrolled it and Gustavo and Kiki leaned in to look. The scroll was covered in very neat, black and red hieroglyphs. There was a drawing of a pyramid at the top, then rows of hieroglyphs beneath. Gustavo recognized a leg, a hippo, and what looked like a pair of doorways.

"What does it say?" asked Kiki.

Bek glanced around, as if he was making sure no one was listening. He whispered, "It's a code. It says where the entrance to Pharaoh Khufu's pyramid is hidden. It must be kept secret, so no one breaks in to steal his treasures."

"What kinds of treasures?" Kiki asked.

"Everything he needs for the afterlife," Bek explained. "Baskets and bowls of food, clothes, jars of wine and oil... Khufu has two boats buried near the pyramid, too."

"Model boats?" said Gustavo. He'd seen pictures of small wooden boats that were buried in ancient Egyptian tombs.

"They're in pieces, but they're full-size ones," said Bek.

"Wow!" said Gustavo and Kiki together.

"There'll be a *lot* of gold and jewels in there, too," said Bek, "and—"

A shadow fell across the doorway. They all turned to see a tall woman wearing a shoulder-length black wig, decorated with beads. A long white shawl hung around her shoulders.

Gustavo drew in a sharp breath. It was the woman

he'd seen hiding behind the statue of Anubis!
I didn't imagine her, he thought.

Behind her was a man wearing a wraparound skirt, like a kilt. There was another woman, too—she wore a long tunic made of rough material. Her hair was short and scruffy.

Bek smiled at the tall woman. "Are you looking for my father?"

"No, I'm not," she replied. She snatched up the papyrus from the table, sending the stones tumbling.

One of them landed on the man's foot. He yelped in pain.

"Quiet, Yuf!" The woman waved the papyrus in Bek's face. "This is what I want—the instructions for getting into the pyramid!"

The scruffy woman giggled. "We're going to get the treasure! We're going to get the treasure!" she chanted.

"Bunefer!" the tall woman snapped. "Cut it out!"

Gustavo leaped forward to snatch back the papyrus. But the woman whipped it aside and pushed past him.

"Yuf! Bunefer! Let's go," she called.

"Yes, Nebet. Coming, Nebet," said the man.

The scruffy woman glared at Gustavo. "Don't follow us, or..."

"Right now, Bunefer!" Nebet shouted.

And they were gone.

Bek looked horrified. "Now they can get into Pharaoh Khufu's tomb and steal his treasures. It's all my fault!"

"You couldn't help it," Kiki said gently.

"You don't understand," said Bek. His eyes were wide with worry. "If anyone finds out they've got that papyrus, Grandpa will be in big trouble."

"Bek!" a voice called. "Bek, I need your help moving these jars!"

"That's him now," said Bek. "What if he finds out the papyrus has been stolen?"

Kiki squeezed his arm. "Go and help your grandpa," she said. "We'll fix this."

"Thank you," Bek said. "May the gods bring you luck!" He disappeared into the next room.

Kiki and Gustavo huddled together.

"Now we know what our mission is," Gustavo whispered excitedly. "We must stop that robbery, so the treasures stay safely in the tomb!"

"Yes!" said Kiki. "Then one day archaeologists can discover them, and they can be displayed in the museum. Imagine how many people will go to see them!"

Gustavo nodded. "We must save those treasures—and help Bek!"

Chapter Four
THE SECRET CODE

Gustavo and Kiki hurried back toward the pyramids. Gustavo gazed up at the largest one and thought of the incredible treasures hidden inside it. He and Kiki were the only ones who could stop Nebet and her gang from stealing them all. It seemed impossible.

"How do we even begin to stop the robbers?" he wondered.

"We need help," Kiki said. "Let's ask the Secret Explorers!"

They headed toward the Nile. Gustavo caught the scent of honey as they passed a line of donkeys laden with jars. They ran down the riverbank to the Beagle and jumped on board.

As their feet hit the deck, the Beagle beeped.

BIP-BIP-BIP-BIP! BIP-BIP!

Gustavo laughed. "We're pleased to see you, too!"

Kiki opened the box that held the communications equipment. As the screen burst into life, she spoke into the mic. "The Beagle to Exploration Station. Can you hear us?"

"Exploration Station to the Beagle. Tamiko here. Sending visual."

The screen flickered and all the Secret Explorers appeared on it.

The sight of their friends immediately made Gustavo feel more hopeful. He quickly explained what had happened. "So to save the museum, we must stop the robbers and make sure no one steals Khufu's treasures," he finished.

"Leah's calling up some pyramid info on her computer," said Cheng.

A moment later, Leah said, "The pyramid has got a few tunnels inside of it. Some of them were possibly built to confuse robbers."

Gustavo nodded. "I remember reading about that. When a pyramid is finished being built, the builders block them off with rubble," he said. "That's to stop robbers getting in."

"I know!" said Connor. "Could you use rubble to seal up the treasure chamber?"

"That would work!" said Gustavo.

Kiki broke in. "We could stick the rubble

together with the mortar the builders use," she said. "If we build a wall across the treasure chamber entrance, the tomb will be safe."

"Great idea!" said Ollie. "But how are you going to get inside the pyramid? The entrance is secret, isn't it?"

Everybody at the Exploration Station turned to their computers, searching for a solution to the problem.

"Hold on," Gustavo said slowly. "You know that papyrus the gang stole? The one with the directions to the secret entrance? I think I remember the hieroglyphs on it. If we can figure out what the code is..."

"Describe them," said Tamiko. "We'll look them up and translate."

"The first one's easy—that was the Sphinx," said Gustavo. "Then it was a sky with a star hanging from it..."

Tamiko's keyboard clacked. "That must mean sunset," she said.

"Then a pair of legs," Gustavo continued. "Then a... squiggly thing..."

"Like a question mark," Kiki chimed in, "but the wrong way around."

"The legs mean walk, and the curly thing's a hundred," said Tamiko. "It must mean walk a hundred paces."

"There was a hippopotamus, too," said Gustavo. "What can that mean?"

"I would guess it means hippopotamus," said Tamiko with a giggle.

"I remember a yellow circle as well," said Kiki, "with lines coming down from it."

"Sunbeams," said Tamiko.

"But it was sort of crossed out," Kiki added.

"Oh. Maybe it was a mistake," said Tamiko.

"Then there was a person looking up," said Gustavo.

Tamiko frowned. "Hmm. Maybe it means you're supposed to look up, too," she said.

"The last ones looked like two doorways,"

remembered Kiki. "Maybe that means the way into the pyramid?"

Tamiko typed quickly. "I think each doorway shape means the number ten," she said. "So both together mean twenty."

"I think that was all of them," said Gustavo. "Can you tell us them again?"

Tamiko took a deep breath. "Sphinx, sunset, walk a hundred paces, hippopotamus, crossed-out sunbeams, a person looking up, and the number twenty," she said.

"Thanks, Tamiko!" said Kiki.

"Thanks, everyone!" Gustavo added. "Beagle out."

"Good luck!" their friends called, then the screen went blank once more. Gustavo hid the communications box under the wooden bench.

BEEP BEEP BEEP! went the Beagle.

"I think it's wishing us good luck, too," said Gustavo with a grin. "Thanks, Beagle!"

They jumped onto the shore. "We need to buy some mortar," said Kiki. Then her face fell. "We haven't got any ancient Egyptian money, though."

"They didn't use money," Gustavo said, as they scrambled up the bank toward the pyramids. "They swapped things instead."

"We haven't got anything to swap either," said Kiki.

Gustavo grinned. "We have—the incense Bek gave you!"

They came to a row of small houses.

Some had mats outside where the owner sat with goods for sale. Outside a bigger house, a merchant was stacking building materials. "Let's try him," Gustavo said.

He asked for mortar, and offered the incense in exchange. The merchant's face lit up. "My daughter will love it," he said, handing Kiki a bulging sack. "It's her favorite scent."

The sun was going down as Kiki and Gustavo headed past the Sphinx. They stood

behind it, facing Pharaoh Khufu's pyramid. To Gustavo's dismay, he realized that the men standing around its base were armed with thick, heavy clubs. Several had daggers tucked into their kilts.

"I don't want to see anyone slacking off!" a broad man was yelling at them. He carried a spear. "Don't let anyone near this pyramid!"

"Oh no!" said Kiki. "How can we get in without being seen?"

"We'll think of something," said Gustavo,

and then he felt his heart sink. Heading toward the boss guard was Nebet. Yuf stumbled along after her, clutching a large bundle of poles. Bunefer followed—she had a coil of rope over her shoulder and a pottery lamp in her hand. Kiki grabbed Gustavo's arm and pulled him into the shadow of the Sphinx, where they were out of sight.

Nebet's voice carried in the still air. "Officer, I'd like you to make the guards go away."

The boss laughed. "Oh, you would, would you? And I'd like to be Egypt's next pharaoh!"

"I'm serious," Nebet said. "Will this change your mind?"

She handed him something that sparkled in the setting sun.

"Jewels," Kiki whispered.

The boss grinned. "Guards! Let's take a nice, long break!"

The guards started to march away. The boss guard followed, and called back to Nebet over his shoulder. "Thanks for the jewels! But there's no way you guys will be able to fit through the tunnels, not with all the rubble in there. You're far too big!"

"Kiki, I *think* I know how to get into the pyramid," said Gustavo. "It's risky, though."

"I'm up for anything that will save the museum," Kiki replied. "What's your idea?"

"No time to explain," said Gustavo. "Just trust me."

They walked toward the gang. Gustavo felt jittery with nerves. *I've got to get this right*, he thought.

Nebet's eyes narrowed. "You two again! What do you want?"

Gustavo took a deep breath. "We know you're tomb robbers," he said.

Nebet laughed. "And you think you can stop us, do you?"

"No," Gustavo replied. "We want to help you."

Chapter Five
A RISKY PLAN

Nebet scowled. "Why would you two want to help us? We know you're friends with the mummifier's grandson." She glanced down at the sack of mortar. "And what's that?"

"Er..." said Gustavo. *This isn't going well*, he thought.

To his relief, Kiki stepped in. "Remember

when you stole the papyrus?" asked Kiki. "Well, we were trying to steal it, too."

"Yes, that's right!" said Gustavo. "And this sack of mortar is to... er... seal up the tomb. After we've stolen the treasures, of course."

Kiki nodded. "Then no one will know they're gone. So that means no one will be looking for us robbers, right?"

Nebet's cold eyes flickered from Gustavo to Kiki. Gustavo could see that she still hadn't made up her mind about them. His heart was pounding. *We've got to convince her she*

needs our help!

"That guard was right," he said. "You and your gang could never squeeze past the rubble. But Kiki and I are much smaller. We can do it! All we want in return is a bit of the treasure. Deal?"

Nebet frowned—and then a greedy grin spread over her face. "All right," she agreed. "Deal."

Yuf and Bunefer cheered. "Yeah, yeah, yeah!"

"But just a *tiny* bit of treasure—that's all you'll get," said Nebet. "And I'll be watching you. Make one wrong move..."

"We won't," Gustavo said firmly.

Yuf and Bunefer danced around each other. "Now we don't have to go into the scary pyramid," said Yuf. "These two kids can do it!"

"Silence!" ordered Nebet with a stare. They immediately fell quiet. Nebet reached into the folds of her shawl and drew out the stolen papyrus. She unrolled it. "Now we must find the entrance..." Nebet stared at the hieroglyph code, muttering to herself. Finally she said, "Stupid thing! It doesn't make any sense."

Bunefer peered at it over her shoulder.

"You've probably got it upside down."

Nebet turned the papyrus the other way up, then glared at Bunefer. "Silly fool! Whoever heard of a pyramid with the pointy part at the bottom!"

"H-have you tried it sideways?" Yuf asked.

Nebet closed her eyes. She looked as if she was about to bite Yuf's head off.

"Let us try," Gustavo said quickly. *Maybe Nebet and her gang can't read*, he thought. He knew that only a small number of ancient Egyptians could.

Nebet passed the papyrus to him. She crossed her arms and tapped her feet on the dusty ground while Gustavo and Kiki examined the hieroglyphs.

Kiki whispered, "Can you remember what Tamiko said they meant?"

"I think so," said Gustavo. "Sphinx, sunset, walk one hundred paces, hippopotamus, crossed-out sunbeams, a person looking up, twenty."

Kiki looked around. "Well, the Sphinx is behind us now. And it's sunset. Let's try walking a hundred paces."

With the robber gang following, Gustavo and Kiki walked, counting as they went.

"Ninety-eight... ninety-nine... one hundred," said Gustavo, stepping on to a low rock that was in his way. He glanced down at the

papyrus. "Next is the hippopotamus. I don't get that. There's no hippo here."

Kiki giggled. "You're standing on it!" she said.

"*What?*" Gustavo quickly looked down, then laughed. The rock he was standing on was shaped exactly like a sleeping hippopotamus.

"Stop messing around," Nebet called. "Get on with it!"

Gustavo checked the papyrus again. "Yellow circle with lines crossed out. Oh, yes— sunbeams." He frowned. "But what does that mean we should do next?"

Kiki thought for a moment. "Maybe it doesn't mean sunbeams... maybe it means where there's no sun... Gustavo, look!"

She pointed to the area in front of the pyramid. It was in deep shadow.

"Amazing, Kiki!" said Gustavo, and they ran over to it.

"Oi! Wait!" shouted Nebet, running after them. Yuf and Bunefer followed her, carrying their ropes and poles.

Gustavo glanced at the papyrus. "Next is the person looking up and the doorways that mean twenty," he said. He looked at the sloping side of the pyramid that rose before them. Excitement bubbled inside of him as

he realized what the instructions meant. "Go up twenty blocks! That's where the secret entrance must be!"

"Awesome!" Kiki exclaimed.

Gustavo rolled up the papyrus and tucked it inside his tunic. They began to climb, using the gaps between the polished stones as hand and footholds. Gustavo could hear Nebet grumbling and Yuf and Bunefer panting for breath as they scrambled up, too. The blocks were huge, and Gustavo thought it was like climing a giant's stairs.

After a while, Kiki stopped. "This is the twentieth block," she said.

Gustavo called down to Nebet. "We think the entrance must be behind this block."

"Up you go, Bunefer," Nebet said. "You're the strongest. Push the stone aside."

Bunefer passed the lighted torch over to Nebet and scrambled up beside Gustavo and Kiki. She gritted aher teeth and pushed the block. Nothing happened. Nebet frowned. "Go and help her, Yuf," she ordered.

Yuf climbed up, too. They both pushed and shoved, then turned and leaned on the block, pushing with their backs. With a loud, scraping noise, the stone block moved. It swiveled sideways, revealing the entrance to a dark tunnel. A moldy smell wafted from inside.

Nebet climbed up and peered in. Her eyes gleamed. "Soon we'll be as rich as the pharaohs!" She lit the pottery lamp and handed it to Gustavo. "Well, what are you waiting for? Get in there!"

"We'll need those, too," Kiki said, pointing at the bundles of ropes and poles.

Bunefer and Yuf gave them to her so fast that Kiki almost dropped them.

"Glad it's you going in and not us," said Yuf. "The gods don't like tombs being disturbed."

"Especially Anubis," said Bunefer. "He'll send evil spirits to get you!"

Gustavo shivered.

"Go on," said Nebet. "Go and fetch my treasure!"

Gustavo took a deep breath. Then he and Kiki stepped into the dark tunnel of Pharaoh Khufu's pyramid...

Chapter Six
INSIDE THE GREAT PYRAMID

Gustavo and Kiki made their way along the dark, stuffy tunnel. They had to stoop to avoid scraping their heads on the rough stone ceiling. Apart from the light flickering from the lamp, it was as dark as the darkest night. Gustavo was glad he didn't believe in Bunefer's evil spirits. *If I did*, he thought, *this would be very creepy.*

The ground sloped steeply downward and they had to be careful not to slip.

"I thought it would be cold in here," Kiki said. "But the farther in we go, the warmer it gets."

"You're right," said Gustavo. He could feel his hair sticking to his damp forehead.

The tunnel flattened out and turned a sharp corner. Then it curved to the left and sloped upward. Ahead, a tall, dark shadow was blocking their way.

"It's rubble left by the pyramid builders," Gustavo said when they reached it. The lamplight showed a huge mound of stones. "It's to stop robbers."

Kiki squashed up beside him. "Do you think it will stop us, too?"

"I'm not sure..." Gustavo held the torch high. "Hey, there's a little gap at the top! Let's see if we can squeeze through it."

Kiki started scrambling up the pile of rubble. Gustavo kept the torch held as high as he could to help her see. Kiki's movements made shadows jump all over the walls of the tunnel. Gustavo waited nervously.

"Just... need... to move... some... of these rocks..." Kiki panted when she reached the top of the pile. "So

we'll... fit through..." There was a crash as she pushed them off the top of the heap.

Gustavo passed the ropes and poles up to Kiki. She pushed them through the gap she'd made, then held the torch so Gustavo could climb up. His sandals slipped on the rocks, but soon he was at the top of the pile of rubble.

"I'll go first," he said, and wriggled into the

gap Kiki had made.

Gustavo felt hot and cramped as he crawled along the top of the rubble, trying not to scrape his head on the tunnel roof. He held the torch in one hand and pulled himself along with the other. "It's tight," he called back to Kiki, "but we can fit through!"

He could hear Kiki starting to crawl after him, pushing the poles and ropes ahead of her. Gustavo was sweltering from the effort. He couldn't help but give a "Whoop!" of relief as he reached the other side of the rubble heap and scrambled down to the ground. Kiki passed him the ropes and poles and jumped down next to him.

"We did it!" said Gustavo. Then he saw that Kiki looked very annoyed. "What's up?"

"Look at that," she said. She pointed ahead of them.

Gustavo groaned. The light from the lamp flickered over a blank wall. "All that effort," said Gustavo, "and it's a dead end."

Kiki laughed. "Well, it is a tomb."

Gustavo moved the torch from side to side. "Hey! It's not a dead-end—it's a junction! The tunnel continues around both corners."

"Which way should we go?" wondered Kiki.

Gustavo peered in each direction. "I think I can see something down here," he said, waving the lamp toward the right-hand tunnel.

They gathered up the poles and ropes and set off down a slope. Gustavo gasped. The thing he'd seen was a white-painted doorway. It was covered in brightly colored hieroglyphics.

"The King's Chamber!" he whispered.

They peered through the doorway and saw a huge carved stone box.

"The Pharaoh's sarcophagus!" said Gustavo. "It's a kind of coffin. Just think, Khufu's mummy is inside that."

"A real pharaoh!" whispered Kiki. "What

are those?" She pointed to several containers next to the sarcophagus.

"Canopic jars!" Gustavo said excitedly. "They hold pieces of his body that were removed before it was mummified." He was trembling with excitement.

Their eyes roved over jeweled chests, golden bowls and cups, baskets of food, jewels, and even games. There were beds and chairs for servants to carry the pharaoh upon.

"Everything Khufu needs in the afterlife," Gustavo said in wonder. He lifted the torch higher. "Look at all the treasure!"

Scattered around the tomb

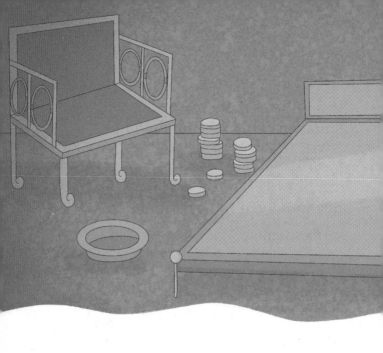

were a collection of incredible objects. There was a bed with a golden canopy, a carrying chair, and thrones covered in gold and jewels.

He noticed some little stone statues standing around the sarcophagus. "Look—shabti figures," he told Kiki. "They're servants. The ancient Egyptians believed they would work for the pharaohs in the afterlife."

Kiki was examining hieroglyphs on the doorway. "Bek could read these," she said. "I wonder what they say."

"They're probably curses, warning thieves to keep out," Gustavo said. "Come on, we can't forget the plan! Let's start moving rubble to the treasure chamber entrance, so we can build a wall."

Back at the junction, Kiki wedged the torch into a gap between stone blocks. She sorted through the poles until she found what she wanted. She looked around until she spotted large cracks high up on each wall. Using the cracks to jam the pole across the tunnel, she flung a rope up so it hung over the pole.

"Tie that end of the rope around a chunk of rock," she said to Gustavo. "I'll pull on the other end, and you can use a pole to push the rock free."

Gustavo did as she asked. As Kiki pulled the rope, he leaned all his weight on the end of the pole.

CRRRRRRKKKK! The rock moved.

"Again!" said Kiki.

The stone shifted free. Gustavo helped Kiki swing it onto the slope that led to the

King's Chamber. The rock rumbled down toward the door.

"Wow!" said Gustavo. "That's a big lump of rock, but we moved it pretty easily."

"That's because we're using the pole as a lever," Kiki explained. "It's doing the work for us." She grinned. "You're not the only history expert around here," she teased. "Did you

know the ancient Egyptians invented levers
and ramps for moving heavy objects?"

"Cool!" said Gustavo.

They carried on moving rubble as fast as
they could.

"We'll soon have enough to block off the
chamber entrance," Gustavo said. "That'll
keep Nebet and her gang out!"

"I knew it!" shrieked a voice, echoing

around the tunnels.

They both froze with horror. It was Nebet!

Kiki's eyes were wide. "She's on the other side of the rubble pile," she whispered.

"Yuf! Bunefer!" Nebet yelled. "Those kids aren't helping us—they're trying to stop us! After them!"

Gustavo grabbed the torch. "Come on, Kiki! Let's run!"

Chapter Seven
TRICKING THE ROBBERS

Gustavo and Kiki sprinted down the left-hand tunnel. It was so narrow that Gustavo could feel his arms brushing the stone walls.

"Get a move on, Yuf!" Nebet's voice echoed. "If Bunefer and I can squeeze over this rubble, so can you."

"They're using the gap we made," said Kiki with dismay.

Then came the crash of falling rocks, a whimper from Yuf, and the sound of lots of pounding feet.

"Quick!" Gustavo said. "They're coming this way!"

Ahead, the torch showed a large alcove in the tunnel wall.

"Here!" Gustavo whispered, pulling Kiki inside the small, cramped space.

"The lamp!" Kiki said. "They'll see us!"

Gustavo dropped the lamp and kicked dust inside it. They were left in total darkness. It was so black that Gustavo couldn't even see the wall. He touched Kiki's shoulder. "Are you okay?" he whispered.

"It's really scary." Her voice shook. "You?"

"It's horrible," he said. "I never imagined anywhere could be this dar–"

He broke off. A light glowed in the blackness.

The light grew brighter. It was Nebet, holding another lamp. It lit up her angry face. She and Bunefer ran past their hiding place, with Yuf puffing along behind. Gustavo's heart pounded so loudly, he was worried they would hear it.

But they didn't. As the gang's footsteps died away, he heard Kiki take a deep, shaky breath.

"Whew!" she said. "We've given them the slip. For now, anyway."

"And we've still got a mission to complete," Gustavo said.

"Right," said Kiki. "Let's try to go back the way we came."

They tiptoed back along the dark tunnel. Kiki kept one hand on Gustavo's shoulder, so they wouldn't get separated. Gustavo felt his way along the wall. He could see nothing but blackness.

Nerves fluttered inside him. *Anything could be waiting for us*, he thought.

FLASH!

A glowing light shone ahead. It lit up the tunnel, dazzling them in the sudden brightness.

Kiki clutched Gustavo's arm. "Nebet's found us!"

"Let's go," Gustavo said. "Quick!"

But then a voice said, "Gustavo? Kiki? Is that you?"

Gustavo blinked. As his eyes grew used to the light, he saw a figure holding a reed torch—and it was too small to be one of the gang. He grinned with relief when he realized who it was. "Bek!"

They rushed to meet him.

"I'm so glad it's you!" said Kiki. "But what are you doing here?"

"I saw the secret door was open, so I came in to try to stop those robbers," said Bek.

The three friends huddled together to decide what to do. Gustavo and Kiki knew their original plan wouldn't work, because the gang would hear them shifting rubble.

"We could scare them away instead," Gustavo suggested. "Just like Bek scared us!"

"But how?" said Kiki. "We don't look scary."

"We don't need to look scary," he said. "Remember Anubis and the bad spirits? I've got an idea that just might work..."

*

"Ready!" said Gustavo.

They were inside the King's Chamber. Around them, the gold and jewels glittered in the light from Bek's torch. Gustavo carefully wedged it between two jars of oil, and ducked down into the shadows. Kiki had rigged up a pulley and was holding the end of a pair of ropes. The other ends were tied around shabti figures.

"Ready!" she called.

Bek was crouched near Gustavo, clutching one of Kiki's incense pellets. "Ready too!" he said.

Gustavo was tense with nerves. He glanced at Khufu's sarcophagus. *I hope you don't mind us being here, Pharaoh,* he thought. *We're trying to save your treasures!*

"They're coming!" Bek hissed.

Gustavo listened. Bek was right—he could hear footsteps outside the chamber and Nebet's angry voice. Then Bunefer gave a yelp. "Treasure!" she screeched. "We've found it!"

Gustavo could just make out the gang all peering through the chamber doorway.

"Wow," said Yuf. "We're rich!"

"As rich as pharaohs," said Nebet. "As long as those kids stay out of the way. Hey, where's that light coming from?"

Bek had picked up the torch, and was dipping its flame to the incense. It lit and he blew on it gently, making smoke rise. Then he tucked the torch back between the jars and scuttled over to Kiki.

Nebet stalked into the chamber, Yuf and Bunefer following. Gustavo gently moved his arms to make the smoke from the incense drift toward the gang.

"What's that?" snapped Nebet.

Yuf and Bunefer looked around nervously. "Smoke," said Yuf. "Ritual smoke. That's not right..."

Kiki and Bek yanked on the ropes.

SCRRRRRRKKKK!

SCRRRRRRKKKK!

Two of the little shabti figures moved along the ground. In the gloomy torchlight, it looked as if they were magically moving all by themselves.

"Yikes!" yelped Yuf.

"Evil spirits!" Bunefer squealed. "Eek! We should never have come here! Run, Yuf!"

They sprinted out of the chamber. Gustavo could hear them scrambling over the rubble pile and racing away toward the secret entrance, their shrieks ringing behind them. He couldn't help but grin!

But Nebet snorted. "Silly kids," she said. "I know it's you. Smelly smoke and a couple of shabti figures don't scare me!" She walked farther into the treasure chamber, toward where Gustavo, Kiki, and Bek were hiding. "Come on, show yourselves!"

Oh no, thought Gustavo. *We've only got one trick left. It's our last chance to save the treasures... and the museum!*

Chapter Eight

HELP FROM ANUBIS

Gustavo crouched low to the ground. He was hidden behind a throne, with Nebet marching toward him. He could see Kiki and Bek hiding behind piles of jewels. The light from Bek's torch flickered over their worried faces.

"Where are you?" growled Nebet.

Gustavo put his hands together with his

thumbs sticking up, and held them upright. The torchlight threw the shadow made by his hands onto the wall in front of Nebet. It was shaped just like the head of a jackal.

Gustavo moved his hands forward. The shadow grew larger.

Nebet stopped and stared, her eyes wide. "Anubis!" she said with a gasp.

355

Gustavo moved his fingers like a pair of scissors, so that the jackal seemed to open and close its jaws.

Nebet shook so hard her shawl fell from her shoulders. "Please don't hurt me, Anubis!" she shrieked. "I wasn't going to steal anything, honestly!"

She turned and fled. Gustavo heard her scramble over the rubble pile, and then her pounding feet echoed through the tunnel as she raced for the exit.

After a couple of moments, the inside of the pyramid was

silent.

"It worked!" Gustavo shouted. "She's gone!"

The cheers of the three friends echoed off the stone walls. Gustavo and Kiki high-fived. "Yay!" shouted Kiki.

Bek looked confused, then stuck his hand up for a high-five as well. He still looked confused after he'd done it!

"Let's seal off that chamber before any of the robbers come back," said Gustavo.

Kiki giggled. "If they dare!"

They carefully placed the shabti figures back where they belonged. Then Kiki showed Gustavo and Bek how to rig up pulleys and levers. It was hard work, but soon they'd shifted almost all the rubble they needed to the doorway.

"Let's get the mortar ready," said Gustavo.

Kiki grabbed the sack, then stopped.

"What's up?" Gustavo asked.

"Water," Kiki said in a small voice. "We need water to mix it and we didn't bring any."

Gustavo groaned. "Oh no!"

But Bek took a stone jar from his bag. "Here," he said.

Gustavo grinned with relief. "Excellent!

Thanks!"

"It's a good thing you sneaked into the pyramid too, Bek," said Kiki.

"Definitely," said Gustavo. "This wouldn't have worked without you!"

They stacked the rubble across the doorway, using the mortar to stick the rocks together. Gradually, Pharaoh Khufu's sarcophagus and his magnificent treasures disappeared from view behind the wall they were building. Between them, Kiki and Bek held Gustavo up on their shoulders so he could slot the last rock into place. He took a last glimpse of the treasure chamber . *I hope no one disturbs it for thousands of years now, he thought.* He fixed the rock in place and the chamber was completely hidden.

Bek put his head on one side. "There's just one more thing," he said, pulling brushes and inks from his bag. He started writing hieroglyphs around the sealed doorway.

"What does it say?" Kiki asked, peering over his shoulder.

Bek grinned. "It's an extra curse," he said. "If you ever meet someone with a bright green nose, very hairy ears, and a voice like a hippo with a tummy ache, you'll know he tried to break down our wall!"

Everyone laughed. As they made their way out of the pyramid, Gustavo spotted something familiar in the torchlight. He picked it up.

"Your grandpa's papyrus with the secret

directions!" he said. "It must have fallen out of my tunic." He passed it to Bek.

Bek shook his head. "Please can you keep it?" he asked. "If you take it back home to Discoveria, none of the robbers around here will ever get hold of it."

"Of course we will," said Gustavo. He put the papyrus back inside his tunic.

When they reached the outside and the cool night air, there was only a crescent moon. No one noticed the three of them heaving the huge block of stone back over the entrance—with the help of Kiki's levers—and then making their way toward the dock.

"Kiki and I had better go home now," said Gustavo.

"You have a long journey ahead," said Bek. "All the way to Discoveria."

"It is quite a journey," Gustavo agreed, "but it shouldn't take too long." Kiki gave him a grin.

When they reached the Beagle, Bek said, "Thanks for everything you've done. My grandpa would be grateful too, if he knew."

"It was a great adventure," said Kiki.

Gustavo made a fist and held it out. "Fist

bump?" he said.

Bek made a fist, too. "Fist bump," he said. "I guess that must mean goodbye."

When they'd all bumped fists, Gustavo and Kiki jumped aboard the Beagle. Gustavo grabbed the oars, and Kiki set the sail. Bek gave the boat a shove away from the dock, then waved as they moved off.

"Bye, Bek!" Gustavo called.

"You'll be a great scribe!" Kiki added.

Wind filled the sail and they turned to take a last look at the pyramids.

"It's awesome to think we've actually

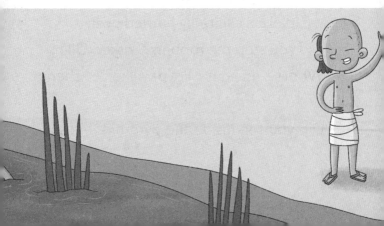

been inside one!" said Gustavo.

When the pyramids were in the far distance, they changed into their ordinary clothes. They sat on the wooden bench and Gustavo pressed the button on the communications box that was marked "HOME".

Dazzling white light surrounded them. The Beagle rattled and shook as it accelerated to an incredible speed. The light faded, and they came to a shuddering standstill. They were back in the Exploration Station once more, and the Beagle had turned back into an old go-kart. The other Secret Explorers excitedly hurried over.

"Did you stop the robbers?" asked Ollie.

"What's ancient Egypt like?" Cheng asked.

"Did you see inside the pyramid?" Roshni

wanted to know.

Before Gustavo and Kiki could answer, a screen projected up from the floor. It showed the museum they'd seen before, but this time it was packed with visitors. They were looking at a reconstruction of Pharaoh Khufu's burial chamber. Gustavo could see jars, treasures and shabtis. *It's exactly what it looked like!* he thought.

Kiki gasped, and pointed to a wall display

next to the chamber. It was headed, "CURSES! CAN YOU GUESS WHAT THEY SAY?" Beside one curse was a figure with a green nose and hairy ears, and it was clutching its stomach. "Bek's curse," said Kiki with a grin, as the screen vanished.

Gustavo grinned, too. Their mission to save the museum had been successful!

"Did you bring anything back for the collection?" asked Leah.

Gustavo carefully pulled the papyrus containing the secret instructions from his pocket. Now it was over four thousand years old, and was faded and fragile.

"I recognize those hieroglyphs," Tamiko

said with a smile. Kiki placed it inside one of the display cabinets.

It was time for Gustavo to go back home.

"What an amazing mission!" Kiki said. She stuck out her fist at exactly the same time as Gustavo high-fived. They both burst out laughing.

"Bye, Kiki!" said Gustavo. "Bye, everyone! See you on our next mission!"

He stepped through the glowing door. The wind whirled him through brilliant white light. When it faded, he stepped out of the elevator and back into the Rio de Janeiro museum. Visitors bustled around him, looking at the exhibits. *The museum in Cairo will be this busy too*, he thought happily.

"Excuse me!"

Gustavo turned to see a smiling elderly man and woman.

"We heard that some of the artifacts in the next gallery are on loan from a museum in Egypt," said the woman. "We were wondering if you could tell us about them."

Gustavo grinned. "Of course," he said. "I happen to know a few things about ancient Egypt!"

GUSTAVO'S MISSION NOTES

THE GREAT PYRAMID OF GIZA

The ancient Egyptians believed that life continued after death. They built pyramids to contain the mummified bodies of their kings— the pharaohs. The mummies were meant to stay in the pyramids forever, while the pharaohs' spirits traveled to the afterlife. There are more than 100 pyramids across Egypt. The biggest is the Great Pyramid of Giza, which is near Cairo. It was built for Pharaoh Khufu.

The stone at the top of a pyramid is called the capstone

Burial chamber of Pharaoh Khufu

The outer layer was made of smooth, white limestone slabs

Rough, dark limestone blocks were used for inner structure

FACT FILE

⚱ Like all the other important tombs of ancient Egypt, it was built on the west bank of the River Nile. The Egyptians believed this was the land of the dead.

* The Great Pyramid was built in
△ 2589 BCE—that's more than 4,500 years ago!

* The Great Pyramid is 482ft tall and made of 2,300,000 blocks of limestone.
△
* It took 20 years to build.

△

Each block weighed as much as an average elephant!

WHO WAS PHARAOH KHUFU?

Khufu was famous for building the Great Pyramid, which is one of the Seven Wonders of the World. But apart from this, we know very little about him. He was the son of Sneferu and Queen Hetepheres I, and is believed to have had three wives.

Khufu had the biggest pyramid, but the only surviving statue of him is tiny—just 3in high.

HOW TO MAKE A MUMMY

The Egyptians believed in an afterlife where they would be reborn as spirits, but only if their bodies were preserved as mummies. Only very rich people could afford this, and it took at least 70 days to mummify a pharaoh. Before reaching the afterlife, the spirits of the dead were thought to travel through an underworld called Duat.

STEP 1 The body was cleaned using water and salt. The internal organs were taken out and placed in special jars.

Canopic jars with the heads of Egyptian gods

STEP 2 The body was filled with bags of salt and left for 40 days to dry out. After, it was stuffed with bandages and spices.

The priests who oversaw mummification wore a mask of the god Anubis

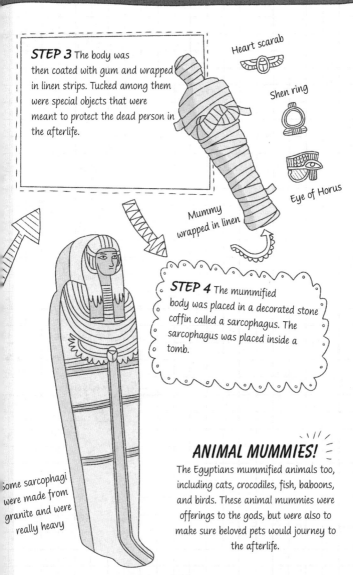

STEP 3 The body was then coated with gum and wrapped in linen strips. Tucked among them were special objects that were meant to protect the dead person in the afterlife.

Heart scarab

Shen ring

Eye of Horus

Mummy wrapped in linen

STEP 4 The mummified body was placed in a decorated stone coffin called a sarcophagus. The sarcophagus was placed inside a tomb.

Some sarcophagi were made from granite and were really heavy

ANIMAL MUMMIES!

The Egyptians mummified animals too, including cats, crocodiles, fish, baboons, and birds. These animal mummies were offerings to the gods, but were also to make sure beloved pets would journey to the afterlife.

GODS AND GODDESSES

Atum-Ra

The father of the gods. Egyptians believed that Atum-Ra created himself and then everything else. He was also one of the gods of the sun.

GOD OF CREATION

Tefnut

GODDESS OF WATER

The daughter of Atum-Ra. Tefnut represented precious water. She was fierce and had the head of a lion.

Horus

GOD OF KINGSHIP

Each new Egyptian pharaoh was believed to be Horus in a different form. He was shown with a falcon's head wearing the crown of Egypt.

Geb

GOD OF EARTH

Geb represented the earth. He was often shown lying flat to support Nut, who represented the sky. The Egyptians believed that earthquakes were caused by Geb laughing.

Ancient Egyptians worshipped gods and goddesses. Some had the heads or bodies of animals. All of the forces of nature, such as the sun, storms, and floods, were represented by a god or goddess.

Osiris
GOD OF THE DEAD

Osiris was Egypt's first king. When he died, he became ruler of the dead and decided who could join him in his underworld kingdom.

Isis
GODDESS OF LIFE

Isis was a powerful magician and one of Egypt's most popular goddesses. She represented magic, fertility, motherhood, death, healing, and rebirth.

Nut
GODDESS OF THE SKY AND STARS

Nut's body was home to the stars and the sun. She was usually shown stretched above Geb.

Anubis
GOD OF EMBALMING

Anubis took care of the bodies of the dead. He created the first mummy from the body of Osiris. He had the head of a jackal—a type of wild dog.

QUIZ

1   What do you call ancient Egyptian writing?

2   Which huge Egyptian statue had a lion's body and a human's face?

3   The pyramids were built on the bank of which river?

4   What were shabti figures?

5   How long did it take to mummify a pharaoh?

6   What was papyrus made from?

7   What was the name of the stone coffin a mummy was placedinside?

8   Which god had a jackal's head?

FIND THE SEA DRAGONS!

There are eight hidden scarabs to spot in this book. Can you find them all?

They look like this!

Check your answers on page 381

GLOSSARY

AFTERLIFE
A second life
that some people
believe will happen
after they die

AMULET
A lucky charm to
protect its owner
from evil

ANCIENT EGYPT
The period between
3100 and 30 BCE,
when Egypt was
ruled by pharaohs

CANOPIC JAR
A special jar used
to store a mummy's
body organs

HIEROGLYPHS
An ancient Egyptian
system of writing
based around
symbols

KHUFU
The pharaoh
responsible for
building the Great
Pyramid of Giza